# Legends of the Hill

**Ruskin Bond** has been writing for over sixty years, and now has over 120 titles in print—novels, collections of short stories, poetry, essays, anthologies and books for children. His first novel, *The Room on the Roof*, received the prestigious John Llewellyn Rhys Prize in 1957. He has also received the Padma Shri (1999), the Padma Bhushan (2014) and two awards from Sahitya Akademi—one for his short stories and another for his writings for children. In 2012, the Delhi government gave him its Lifetime Achievement Award.

Born in 1934, Ruskin Bond grew up in Jamnagar, Shimla, New Delhi and Dehradun. Apart from three years in the UK, he has spent all his life in India, and now lives in Mussoorie with his adopted family.

# RUSKIN BOND

## Legends of the Hill

RUPA

Published by
Rupa Publications India Pvt. Ltd 2021
7/16, Ansari Road, Daryaganj
New Delhi 110002

*Sales centres:*
Allahabad Bengaluru Chennai
Hyderabad Jaipur Kathmandu
Kolkata Mumbai

ISBN: 978-93-91256-83-8

First impression 2021

10 9 8 7 6 5 4 3 2 1

The moral right of the author has been asserted.

# Contents

# Introduction

There is one thing common to all the places of the world—they each have their own stories, legends and mysteries. What makes a destination interesting is not just the sights to see, the monuments to visit, the history to read, but the stories it has collected over time—the stories that have become a part of its people, and its culture. This book is a collection of such stories.

A good mystery can make life interesting. And the hills have a plethora of enticing mysteries. Old, creaky, abandoned homes; a dark forest that no one inhabits but is said to become noisy at night; and all the unique flora and fauna that one will not find anywhere else and have been a part of the hill's legends.

This book tells you the story of Pari Tibba and its relationship with lightning; trains that remind you of dragons; unsolved murder mysteries that are scandalous to the villagers and travellers alike; strangers that leave an everlasting impact on your life. It tells the tale of man-eating panthers, friendly leopards and star-crossed lovers whose spirits roam in a quest to unite with each other. This book is for children and adults alike, all you need is a healthy appetite for intrigue!

Ruskin Bond

# Hill of the Fairies

Fairy Hill, or Pari Tibba as the paharis call it, is a lonely uninhabited mountain lying to the east of Mussoorie, at a height of about 6,000 feet. I have visited it occasionally, scrambling up its rocky slopes where the only paths are the narrow tracks made by goats and the small hill cattle. Rhododendrons and a few stunted oaks are the only trees on the hillsides, but at the summit is a small, grassy plateau ringed by pine trees.

It may have been on this plateau that the early settlers tried building their houses. All their attempts met with failure. The area seemed to attract the worst of any thunderstorm, and several dwellings were struck by lightning and burnt to the ground. People then confined themselves to the adjacent Landour Hill, where a flourishing hill-station soon grew up.

Why Pari Tibba should be struck so often by lightning has always been something of a mystery to me. Its soil and rock seem no different from the soil or rock of any other mountain in the vicinity. Perhaps a geologist can explain the phenomenon; or perhaps it has something to do with the fairies.

'Why do they call it the Hill of the Fairies?' I asked an old resident, a retired schoolteacher. 'Is the place haunted?'

'So they say,' he said.

'Who say?'

'Oh, people who have heard it's haunted. Some years after the site was abandoned by the settlers, two young runaway lovers took shelter for the night in one of the ruins. There was a bad storm and they were struck by lightning. Their charred bodies were found a few days later. They came from different communities and were buried far from each other, but their spirits hold a tryst every night under the pine trees. You might see them if you're on Pari Tibba after sunset.'

There are no ruins on Pari Tibba, and I can only presume that the building materials were taken away for use elsewhere. And I did not stay on the hill till after sunset. Had I tried climbing downhill in the dark, I would probably have ended up as the third ghost on the mountain. The lovers might have resented my intrusion; or, who knows, they might have welcomed a change. After a hundred years together on a windswept mountain-top, even the most ardent of lovers must tire of each other.

Who could have been seeing ghosts on Pari Tibba after sunset? The nearest resident is a woodcutter who makes charcoal at the bottom of the hill. Terraced fields and a small village straddle the next hill. But the only inhabitants of Pari Tibba are the langurs. They feed on oak leaves and rhododendron buds. The rhododendrons contain an intoxicating nectar, and after dining—or wining—to excess, the young monkeys tumble about on the grass in high spirits.

The black bulbuls also feed on the nectar of the rhododendron flower, and perhaps this accounts for the cheekiness of these birds. They are aggressive, disreputable little creatures, who go about in rowdy gangs. The song of most bulbuls consists of several pleasant tinkling notes; but that of the Himalayan black bulbul is as musical as the bray of an ass. Men of science, in their wisdom, have given this bird the sibilant name of *Hypsipetes psaroides*. But the hillmen, in their greater wisdom, call the species the *ban bakra*, which means the 'jungle goat'.

Perhaps the flowers have something to do with the fairy legend. In April and May, Pari Tibba is covered with the dazzling yellow flowers of St. John's Wort (wort meaning herb). The paharis call the flower a wild rose, and it does resemble one. In Ireland it is called the Rose of Sharon.

In Europe this flower is reputed to possess certain magical and curative properties. It is believed to drive away all evil and protect you from witches. But do not tread on St. John's Wort after sunset, lest a fairy horseman come and carry you off, landing you almost anywhere.

By day, St. John's Wort is kindly. Are you insane? Then drink the sap from the leaves of the plant, and you will be cured. Are you hurt? Take the juice and apply it to your wound—and if at first this doesn't help, just keep applying juice until you stop bleeding, or breathing. Are you bald? Then rise early and bathe your head with the dew from St. John's Wort, and your hair will grow again—if you don't catch pneumonia.

Can St. John's Wort be connected with the fairy legend of Pari Tibba? It is said that most flowers, when they die, become fairies. This might be especially true of St. John's Wort.

There is yet another legend connected with the mountain. A shepherd-boy, playing on his flute, discovered a beautiful silver snake basking on a rock. The snake spoke to the boy, saying, 'I was a princess once, but a jealous witch cast a spell over me and turned me into a snake. This spell can only be broken if someone who is pure in heart kisses me thrice. Many years have passed, and I have not been able to find one who is pure in heart.' Then the shepherd-boy took the snake in his arms, and he put his lips to its mouth, and at the third kiss he discovered that he was holding a beautiful princess in his arms. What happened afterwards is anybody's guess.

There are snakes on Pari Tibba, and though they are probably harmless, I have never tried taking one of them in my arms. Once, near a spring, I came upon a checkered water snake. Its body was a series of bulges. I used a stick to exert pressure along the snake's length, and it disgorged five frogs. They came out one after the other, and, to my astonishment, hopped off, little the worse for their harrowing experience. Perhaps they, too, were enchanted. Perhaps shepherd-boys, when they kiss, the snake-princess, are turned into frogs and remain inside the snake's belly until a writer comes along with a magic stick and releases them from bondage.

Biologists probably have their own explanation for the frogs, but I'm all for perpetuating the fairy legends of Pari Tibba.

# Dragon in the Tunnel

The first time I saw a train, I was standing on a wooded slope outside a tunnel, not far from Kalka. Suddenly, with a shrill whistle and great burst of steam, a green and black engine came snorting out of the blackness.

I turned and ran to my father. 'A dragon!' I shouted. 'There's a dragon coming out of its cave!'

Since then, steam engines and dragons have always inspired the same sort of feelings in me—wonder and awe and delight. I would like to see a real dragon one day, green and gold and—because I have always preferred the 'reluctant' sort—rather shy and gentle; but until that day comes, I shall be content with steam engines.

In India the steam engine is still very much with us. In 1855 the East India Railway was opened between Calcutta and Raniganj, a distance of 122 miles. By the turn of the century, India had one of the most extensive railway systems in the world. Today, the hundreds of trains that criss-cross the subcontinent, panting over the desert and plain, through hill and forest, are still pulled by these snorting monsters who belch smoke by day and scatter red stars in the night.

Even now, when I see a train coming around the bend of a hill, on crossing a bridge, or cutting across a wide flat plain,

I feel the same sort of innocent wonder that I felt as a boy. Where are all these people going to, and where have they come from, and what are they really like? When children wave to me from carriage windows I wave back to them. It is a habit I have never lost. And sometimes I am in a train, waving, and the children from the nearby villages come running out of their mud huts to wave back to me—well, not to me exactly, it is really the train they are waving to...

Small wayside stations have always fascinated me. Manned sometimes by just one or two railway employees, and often situated in the middle of a damp subtropical forest, or clinging to the mountainside on the way to Simla or Darjeeling, these little stations are, for me, outposts of romance, lonely symbols of the pioneering spirit that led men to lay tracks into the remote corners of the earth.

I remember such a stop on a line that went through the Terai forests near the foothills of the Himalayas. At about ten at night, the khilasi, or station watchman, lit his kerosene lamp and started walking up the tracks into the jungle.

'Where are you going?' I asked.

'To see if the tunnel is clear,' he said. 'The Overland Mail comes in twenty minutes.'

I accompanied him a furlong or two along the track, through a deep cutting which led to the tunnel. Every night, the khilasi walked through the dark tunnel, and then stood outside to wave his lamp to the oncoming train as a signal that the track was clear. If the engine driver did not see the lamp he stopped the train. It always slowed down near the cutting.

Having inspected the tunnel, we stood outside, waiting for the train. It seemed a long time coming. There was no moon, and the dense forest seemed to be trying to crowd us into the narrow cutting. The sounds of the forest came to us—the belling of a sambhur deer and the cry of a jackal told us that perhaps a tiger or a leopard was on the prowl. There were strange, nocturnal bird sounds; and then silence.

The khilasi stood outside the tunnel, trimming his lamp, listening to the faint sounds of the jungle—sounds which only he could identify and understand. Something made him stand very still for a few moments, peering into the darkness, and I knew that everything was not as it should be.

'There is something in the tunnel,' he said.

I could hear nothing at first, but then there came a regular sawing sound, just like the sound made by someone sawing through the branch of a tree.

'Baghera!' whispered the khilasi. He had said enough to enable me to recognize the sound—the sawing of a leopard trying to find its mate. 'The train will be coming soon. We must drive the animal out, or it will be run over!'

He must have sensed my surprise, because he said, 'Do not be afraid...I know this leopard well. We have seen each other many times. He has a weakness for stray dogs and goats, but he will not harm us.' He gave me his small handaxe to hold and, raising his lamp high, started walking into the tunnel, shouting at the top of his voice to try and scare away the animal. I followed close behind him.

We had gone about twenty yards into the tunnel when the light from the lamp fell on the leopard, which was crouching between the tracks, only about twenty feet away from us. It bared its teeth in a snarl and went down on its stomach, tail twisting. I thought it was going to spring. The khilasi and I both shouted together. Our voices rang and echoed through the tunnel. And the leopard, uncertain as to how many humans were in there with him, turned swiftly and disappeared into the darkness ahead.

The khilasi and I walked on till the end of the tunnel without seeing the leopard again. As we returned to the entrance of the tunnel the rails began to hum and we knew the train was coming.

I put my hand to one of the rails and felt its tremor. And then the engine came round the bend, hissing at us, scattering sparks into the darkness, defying the jungle as it roared through the steep sides of the cutting. It charged straight at the tunnel and into it, thundering past us like the beautiful dragon of my dreams.

And when it had gone, the silence returned and the forest breathed again. Only the rails still trembled with the passing of the train.

# Great Spirits of the Trees

Explore the history and mythology of almost any Indian tree, and you will find that at some point in our civilization it has held an important place in the minds and hearts of the people of this land.

During the rains, when the neem-pods fall and are crushed underfoot, they give out a strong refreshing aroma which lingers in the air for days. This is because the neem gives out more oxygen than most trees. When the ancient herbalists held that the neem was a great purifier of the air, and that its leaves, bark and sap had medicinal qualities, they were quite right, for the neem is still used in medicine today.

From the earliest times it was connected with the gods who protect us from disease. Some castes regarded the tree as sacred to Sitala, the smallpox goddess. When children fell ill, a branch of the neem was waved over them. The tree is said to have sprung from the nectar of the gods, and people still chew the leaves as a means of purification, both spiritual and physical. The tree is also connected with the sun, as in the story of neem-barak, 'The Sun in the Neem Tree'. The sun-god invited to dinner a man of the Bairagi tribe whose rules forbade him to eat except by daylight. Dinner was late, and as darkness fell, the Bairagi feared he would have to go hungry.

But Suraj Narayan, the sun-god, descended from a neem tree and continued shining till dinner was over.

Why have so many trees been held sacred, not only in India but the world over?

To early man they were objects of awe and wonder. The mystery of their growth, the movement of their leaves and branches, the way they seemed to die and then come to life again in spring, the growth of the plant from the seed, all these happenings appeared as miracles—as indeed they are! And because of the wonderful growth of a tree, people began to suppose that it was occupied by spirits, and devotion to a tree became devotion to the spirit or tree-god who occupied it. In *Puck of Pook's Hill,* Kipling wove some wonderful stories, around Puck, the tree-spirit, and the sacred trees of Old England—oak, ash and thorn: 'I came into England with Oak, Ash, and Thorn, and when Oak, Ash and Thorn are gone, I shall go too.'

Among the Gonds of Central India, before a man cut a tree he had to beg its pardon for the injury he was about to inflict on it. He would not shake a tree at night because the tree-spirit was asleep and might be disturbed. When a tree had to be felled, the Gonds would pour ghee on the stump, saying: 'Grow thou out of this, O Lord of the Forest, grow into a hundred shoots! May we grow with a thousand shoots.'

The beautiful mahua is a forest tree held sacred by a number of tribes. Early on the wedding morning, before he goes to fetch his bride, the Bagdi bridegroom goes through a mock marriage with a mahua tree. He embraces it and daubs it with vermilion, his right wrist is bound to it with thread, and after he is released from the tree the thread is used to attach a bunch of mahua leaves to his wrist.

There is a beautiful tradition connected with the sal tree. It is said that at the time of the Buddha's birth, his mother stretched out her hand to take hold of a branch of the sal and he was delivered. Sal trees are also said to have rendered homage to the Buddha at his death, letting fall on him their flowers out of season, and bending their branches to shade him.

Special respect is paid to trees growing near the graves of Muslim saints. Near the tomb of a famous saint, Musa Sohag, at Ahmedabad, there used to be a large old champa tree—perhaps it is still there—the branches of which were hung with glass bangles. Those anxious to have children came and offered bangles to the saint—the number of bangles depending on the means of the supplicant. If the saint favoured a wish, the champa tree 'snatched up the bangles and wore them on its arms'.

Another spectacular tree which has its place in our folklore is the dhak, or palasa, which gave its name to the battlefield of Plassey. It has the habit of dropping its leaves when it flowers, the upper and outer branches standing out in sprays of scarlet and orange. The flowers are sometimes used to dye the powder scattered at Holi, the spring festival; and the wood, said to contain the seed of fire, is used in lighting the Holi bonfire. Legend tells us that the sun-god aimed an arrow at earth, and that it took root and became the palasa tree.

The babul (or keekar) is not very impressive to look at but it will grow almost anywhere in the plains, and there are a number of old beliefs associated with it. For instance, you can cure fever and headache at a babul tree if you tie seven cotton threads from your left big toe to your head, and from your head to a branch of the tree. Then you must embrace the trunk seven times. Try it sometime. You will be so busy tying threads that you will forget you ever had a headache! And there are no after-effects.

Another belief concerning the babul is that if you water it regularly for thirteen days, you acquire control over the spirit who occupies it. There is a story about a man in Saharanpur who did this, and when he died and his corpse was taken away for cremation, no sooner was his pyre lit than he got up and walked away!

In the folklore of India, the mango is the 'wish-fulfilling tree'. When you want to make a wish on a mango tree, shut your eyes and get someone to lead you to the tree; then rub mango blossoms in your hands, and make your wish. The favour granted lasts only for a year, and the charm must be performed again at the next flowering of the tree. In the spring, the young leaves and buds symbolize the darts of Manmatha, or Kamadeva, God of Love.

Another 'wishing tree', the kalp-vriksha, is an enormous old mulberry that is still cared for at Joshimath in Garhwal. It is said to be the tree beneath which the great Sankaracharya often meditated during his sojourn in the Himalayas. Judging by its girth, it might well be over a thousand years old.

Whole forests have been held sacred, such as that in Berar which was dedicated to a particular temple; no one dared to buy or cut the trees. The sacred groves near Mathura, where Lord Krishna sported as a youth, were also protected for centuries. But now, alas, even the hallowed groves are disappearing, making way for the demands of an ever-increasing population. A pity, because every human needs a tree of his own. Even if you do not worship the tree-spirit, you can love the tree.

# The Trouble with Jinns

My friend Jimmy has only one arm. He lost the other when he was a young man of twenty-five. The story of how he lost his good right arm is a little difficult to believe, but I swear that it is absolutely true.

To begin with, Jimmy was (and presumably still is) a Jinn. Now a Jinn isn't really a human like us. A Jinn is a spirit creature from another world who has assumed, for a lifetime, the physical aspect of a human being. Jimmy was a true Jinn and he had the Jinn's gift of being able to elongate his arm at will. Most Jinns can stretch their arms to a distance of twenty or thirty feet. Jimmy could attain forty feet. His arm would move through space or up walls or along the ground like a beautiful gliding serpent. I have seen him stretched out beneath a mango tree, helping himself to ripe mangoes from the top of the tree. He loved mangoes. He was a natural glutton and it was probably his gluttony that first led him to misuse his peculiar gifts.

We were at school together at a hill station in northern India. Jimmy was particularly good at basketball. He was clever enough not to lengthen his arm too much because he did not want anyone to know that he was a Jinn. In the boxing ring he generally won his fights. His opponents never seemed to get past his amazing reach. He just kept tapping them on the nose until they retired from the ring bloody and bewildered.

It was during the half-term examinations that I stumbled on Jimmy's secret. We had been set a particularly difficult algebra paper but I had managed to cover a couple of sheets with correct answers and was about to forge ahead on another sheet when I noticed someone's hand on my desk. At first I thought it was the invigilator's. But when I looked up there was no one beside me.

Could it be the boy sitting directly behind? No, he was engrossed in his question paper and had his hands to himself. Meanwhile, the hand on my desk had grasped my answer sheets and was cautiously moving off. Following its descent, I found that it was attached to an arm of amazing length and pliability. This moved stealthily down the desk and slithered across the floor, shrinking all the while, until it was restored to its normal length. Its owner was of course one who had never been any good at algebra.

I had to write out my answers a second time but after the exam I went straight up to Jimmy, told him I didn't like his game and threatened to expose him. He begged me not to let anyone know, assured me that he couldn't really help himself, and offered to be of service to me whenever I wished. It was tempting to have Jimmy as my friend, for with his long reach he would obviously be useful. I agreed to overlook the matter of the pilfered papers and we became the best of pals.

It did not take me long to discover that Jimmy's gift was more of a nuisance than a constructive aid. That was because Jimmy had a second-rate mind and did not know how to make proper use of his powers. He seldom rose above the trivial. He used his long arm in the tuck shop, in the classroom, in the dormitory. And when we were allowed out to the cinema, he used it in the dark of the hall.

Now the trouble with all Jinns is that they have a weakness for women with long black hair. The longer and blacker the hair, the better for Jinns. And should a Jinn manage to take possession of the woman he desires, she goes into a decline and her beauty decays. Everything about her is destroyed except for the beautiful long black hair.

Jimmy was still too young to be able to take possession in this way, but he couldn't resist touching and stroking long black hair. The cinema was the best place for the indulgence of his whims. His arm would start stretching, his fingers would feel their way along the rows of seats and his lengthening limb would slowly work its way along the aisle until it reached the back of the seat in which sat the object of his admiration. His hand would stroke the long black hair with great tenderness and if the girl felt anything and looked round, Jimmy's hand would disappear behind the seat and lie there poised like the hood of a snake, ready to strike again.

At college two or three years later, Jimmy's first real victim succumbed to his attentions. She was a lecturer in economics, not very good looking, but her hair, black and lustrous, reached almost to her knees. She usually kept it in plaits but Jimmy saw her one morning just after she had taken a head bath, and her hair lay spread out on the cot on which she was reclining. Jimmy could no longer control himself. His spirit, the very essence of his personality, entered the woman's body and the next day she was distraught, feverish and excited. She would not eat, went into a coma, and in a few days dwindled to a mere skeleton. When she died, she was nothing but skin and bone but her hair had lost none of its loveliness.

I took pains to avoid Jimmy after this tragic event. I could not prove that he was the cause of the lady's sad demise but in my own heart I was quite certain of it. For since meeting Jimmy, I had read a good deal about Jinns and knew their ways.

We did not see each other for a few years. And then, holidaying in the hills last year, I found we were staying at the same hotel. I could not very well ignore him and after we had drunk a few beers together I began to feel that I had perhaps misjudged Jimmy and that he was not the irresponsible Jinn I had taken him for. Perhaps the college lecturer had died of some mysterious malady that attacks only college lecturers and Jimmy had nothing at all to do with it.

We had decided to take our lunch and a few bottles of beer to a grassy knoll just below the main motor road. It was late afternoon and I had been sleeping off the effects of the beer when I woke to find Jimmy looking rather agitated.

'What's wrong?' I asked.

'Up there, under the pine trees,' he said. 'Just above the road. Don't you see them?'

'I see two girls,' I said. 'So what?'

'The one on the left. Haven't you noticed her hair?'

'Yes, it is very long and beautiful and—now look, Jimmy, you'd better get a grip on yourself!' But already his hand was out of sight, his arm snaking up the hillside and across the road.

Presently I saw the hand emerge from some bushes near the girls and then cautiously make its way to the girl with the black tresses. So absorbed was Jimmy in the pursuit of his favourite pastime that he failed to hear the blowing of a horn. Around the bend of the road came a speeding Mercedes Benz truck.

Jimmy saw the truck but there wasn't time for him to shrink his arm back to normal. It lay right across the entire width of the road and when the truck had passed over it, it writhed and twisted like a mortally wounded python.

By the time the truck driver and I could fetch a doctor, the arm (or what was left of it) had shrunk to its ordinary size. We took Jimmy to hospital where the doctors found it necessary to amputate. The truck driver, who kept insisting that the arm he ran over was at least thirty feet long, was arrested on a charge of drunken driving.

Some weeks later I asked Jimmy, 'Why are you so depressed? You still have one arm. Isn't it gifted in the same way?'

'I never tried to find out,' he said, 'and I'm not going to try now.'

He is, of course, still a Jinn at heart and whenever he sees a girl with long black hair he must be terribly tempted to try out his one good arm and stroke her beautiful tresses. But he has learnt his lesson. It is better to be a human without any gifts than a Jinn or a genius with one too many.

# Some Hill Station Ghosts

Shimla has its phantom-rickshaw and Lansdowne its headless horseman. Mussoorie has its woman in white. Late at night, she can be seen sitting on the parapet wall on the winding road up to the hill station. Don't stop to offer her a lift. She will fix you with her evil eye and ruin your holiday.

The Mussoorie taxi drivers and other locals call her Bhoot Aunty. Everyone has seen her at some time or the other. To give her a lift is to court disaster. Many accidents have been attributed to her baleful presence. And when people pick themselves up from the road (or are picked up by concerned citizens), Bhoot Aunty is nowhere to be seen, although survivors swear that she was in the car with them.

Ganesh Saili, Abha and I were coming back from Dehradun late one night when we saw this woman in white sitting on the parapet by the side of the road. As our headlights fell on her, she turned her face away, Ganesh, being a thorough gentleman, slowed down and offered her a lift. She turned towards us then, and smiled a wicked smile. She seemed quite attractive except that her canines protruded slightly in vampire fashion.

'Don't stop!' screamed Abha. 'Don't even look at her! It's Aunty!'

Ganesh pressed down on the accelerator and sped past her.

Next day we heard that a tourist's car had gone off the road and the occupants had been severely injured. The accident took place shortly after they had stopped to pick up a woman in white who had wanted a lift. But she was not among the injured.

◆

Miss Ripley-Bean, an old English lady who was my neighbour when I lived near Wynberg-Allen school, told me that her family was haunted by a malignant phantom head that always appeared before the death of one of her relatives.

She said her brother saw this apparition the night before her mother died, and both she and her sister saw it before the death of their father. The sister slept in the same room. They were both awakened one night by a curious noise in the cupboard facing their beds. One of them began getting out of bed to see if their cat was in the room, when the cupboard door suddenly opened and a luminous head appeared. It was covered with matted hair and appeared to be in an advanced stage of decomposition. Its fleshless mouth grinned at the terrified sisters. And then as they crossed themselves, it vanished. The next day they learned that their father, who was in Lucknow, had died suddenly, at about the time that they had seen the death's head.

◆

Everyone likes to hear stories about haunted houses; even sceptics will listen to a ghost story, while casting doubts on its veracity.

Rudyard Kipling wrote a number of memorable ghost stories set in India—*Imray's Return, The Phantom Rickshaw, The Mark of the Beast, The End of the Passage*—his favourite milieu being the haunted dak bungalow. But it was only after his return to

England that he found himself actually having to live in a haunted house. He writes about it in his autobiography, *Something of Myself.*

> The spring of '96 saw us in Torquay, where we found a house for our heads that seemed almost too good to be true. It was large and bright, with big rooms each and all open to the sun, the ground embellished with great trees and the warm land dipping southerly to the clean sea under the Mary Church cliffs. It had been inhabited for thirty years by three old maids.
>
> The revelation came in the shape of a growing depression which enveloped us both—a gathering blackness of mind and sorrow of the heart, that each put down to the new, soft climate and, without telling the other, fought against for long weeks. It was the Feng-shui—the Spirit of the house itself—that darkened the sunshine and fell upon us every time we entered, checking the very words on our lips... We paid forfeit and fled. More than thirty years later we returned down the steep little road to that house, and found, quite unchanged, the same brooding spirit of deep despondency within the rooms.

Again, thirty years later, he returned to this house in his short story, 'The House Surgeon', in which two sisters cannot come to terms with the suicide of a third sister, and brood upon the tragedy day and night until their thoughts saturate every room of the house.

Many years ago, I had a similar experience in a house in Dehradun, in which an elderly English couple had died from neglect and starvation. In 1947, when many European residents were leaving the town and emigrating to the UK, this poverty-stricken old couple, sick and friendless, had been forgotten. Too ill to go out for food or medicine, they had died in their beds, where they were discovered several days later by the landlord's munshi.

The house stood empty for several years. No one wanted to live in it. As a young man, I would sometimes roam about the neglected grounds or explore the cold, bare rooms, now stripped of furniture, doorless and windowless, and I would be assailed by a feeling of deep gloom and depression. Of course I knew what had happened there, and that may have contributed to the effect the place had on me. But when I took a friend, Jai Shankar, through the house, he told me he felt quite sick with apprehension and fear. 'Ruskin, why have you brought me to this awful house?' he said. 'I'm sure it's haunted.' And only then did I tell him about the tragedy that had taken place within its walls.

Today, the house is used as a government office. No one lives in it at night except for a Gurkha chowkidar, a man of strong nerves who sleeps in the back veranda. The atmosphere of the place doesn't bother him, but he does hear strange sounds in the night. 'Like someone crawling about on the floor above,' he tells me. 'And someone groaning. These old houses are noisy places...'

◆

A morgue is not a noisy place, as a rule. And for a morgue attendant, corpses are silent companions.

Old Mr Jacob, who lives just behind the cottage, was once a morgue attendant for the local mission hospital. In those days it was situated at Sunny Bank, about a hundred metres up the hill from here. One of the outhouses served as the morgue: Mr Jacob begs me not to identify it.

He tells me of a terrifying experience he went through when he was doing night duty at the morgue.

'The body of a young man was found floating in the Aglar River, behind Landour, and was brought to the morgue while I was on night duty. It was placed on the table and covered with a sheet.

'I was quite accustomed to seeing corpses of various kinds and did not mind sharing the same room with them, even after dark. On this occasion a friend had promised to join me, and to pass the time I strolled around the room, whistling a popular tune. I think it was "Danny Boy", if I remember right. My friend was a long time coming, and I soon got tired of whistling and sat down on the bench beside the table. The night was very still, and I began to feel uneasy. My thoughts went to the boy who had drowned and I wondered what he had been like when he was alive. Dead bodies are so impersonal...

'The morgue had no electricity, just a kerosene lamp, and after some time I noticed that the flame was very low. As I was about to turn it up, it suddenly went out. I lit the lamp again, after extending the wick. I returned to the bench, but I had not been sitting there for long when the lamp again went out, and something moved very softly and quietly past me.

'I felt quite sick and faint, and could hear my heart pounding away. The strength had gone out of my legs, otherwise I would have fled from the room. I felt quite weak and helpless, unable even to call out.

'Presently the footsteps came nearer and nearer. Something cold and icy touched one of my hands and felt its way up towards my neck and throat. It was behind me, then it was before me. Then it was *over* me. I was in the arms of the corpse!

'I must have fainted, because when I woke up I was on the

floor, and my friend was trying to revive me. The corpse was back on the table.'

'It may have been a nightmare,' I suggested. 'Or you allowed your imagination to run riot.'

'No,' said Mr Jacobs. 'There were wet, slimy marks on my clothes. And the feet of the corpse matched the wet footprints on the floor.'

After this experience, Mr Jacobs refused to do any more night duty at the morgue.

◆

From Herbertpur near Paonta you can go up to Kalsi, and then up the hill road to Chakrata.

Chakrata is in a security zone, most of it off limits to tourists, which is one reason why it has remained unchanged in 150 years of its existence. This small town's population of 1,500 is the same today as it was in 1947—probably the only town in India that hasn't shown a population increase.

Courtesy a government official, I was fortunate enough to be able to stay in the forest rest house on the outskirts of the town. This is a new building, the old rest house—a little way downhill—having fallen into disuse. The chowkidar told me the old rest house was haunted, and that this was the real reason for its having been abandoned. I was a bit sceptical about this, and asked him what kind of haunting took place in it. He told me that he had himself gone through a frightening experience in the old house, when he had gone there to light a fire for some forest officers who were expected that night. After lighting the fire, he looked round and saw a large black animal, like a wild cat, sitting on the wooden floor and gazing into the fire. 'I called out to it, thinking it was someone's pet. The creature turned, and looked full at me with eyes that were human, and a face which was the face of an ugly woman. The creature snarled at me, and the snarl became an angry howl. Then it vanished!'

'And what did you do?' I asked.

'I vanished too,' said the chowkidar. 'I haven't been down to that house again.'

I did not volunteer to sleep in the old house but made myself comfortable in the new one, where I hoped I would not be troubled by any phantom. However, a large rat kept me company, gnawing away at the woodwork of a chest of drawers. Whenever I switched on the light it would be silent, but as soon as the light was off, it would start gnawing away again.

This reminded me of a story old Miss Kellner (of my Dehra childhood) told me, of a young man who was desperately in love with a girl who did not care for him. One day, when he was following her in the street, she turned on him and, pointing to a rat which some boys had just killed, said, 'I'd as soon marry that rat as marry you.' He took her cruel words so much to heart that he pined away and died. After his death the girl was haunted at night by a rat and occasionally she would be bitten. When the family decided to emigrate, they travelled down to Bombay in order to embark on a ship sailing for London. The ship had just left the quay, when shouts and screams were heard from the pier. The crowd scattered, and a huge rat with fiery eyes ran down to the end of the quay. It sat there, screaming with rage, then jumped into the water and disappeared. After that (according to Miss Kellner), the girl was not haunted again.

Old dak bungalows and forest rest houses have a reputation for being haunted. And most hill stations have their resident ghosts—and ghost writers! But I will not extend this catalogue of ghostly hauntings and visitations, as I do not want to discourage tourists from visiting Landour and Mussoorie. In some countries, ghosts are an added attraction for tourists. Britain boasts of hundreds of haunted castles and stately homes, and visitors to Romania seek out Transylvania and Dracula's castle. So do we promote Bhoot Aunty as a tourist attraction? Only if she reforms and stops sending vehicles off those hairpin bends that lead to Mussoorie.

# A Demon for Work

In a village in South India there lived a very rich landlord who owned several villages and many fields; but he was such a great miser that he found it difficult to find tenants who would willingly work on his land, and those who did, gave him a lot of trouble. As a result, he left all his fields unfilled, and even his tanks and water channels dried up. This made him poorer day by day. But he made no effort to obtain the goodwill of his tenants.

One day, a holy man paid him a visit. The landlord poured out his tale of woe.

'These miserable tenants won't do a thing for me,' he complained. 'All my lands are going to waste.'

'My dear good landlord,' said the holy man. 'I think I can help you, if you will repeat a mantra—a few magic words—which I will teach you. If you repeat it for three months, day and night, a wonderful demon will appear before you on the first day of the fourth month. He will willingly be your servant and take upon himself all the work that has been left undone by your wretched tenants. The demon will obey all your orders. You will find him equal to a hundred servants!'

The miserly landlord immediately fell at the feet of the holy man and begged for instruction. The sage gave him the magic words and then went his way. The landlord, greatly pleased, repeated the mantra day and night, for three months, till, on the first day of the fourth month, a magnificent young demon stood before him.

'What can I do for you, master?' he said. 'I am at your command.'

The landlord was taken aback by the sight of the huge monster who stood before him, and by the sound of his terrible voice, but he summoned up enough courage to say, 'You can work for me provided—er—you don't expect any salary.'

'Very well,' said the demon, 'but I have one condition. You must give me enough work to keep me busy all the time. If I have nothing to do, I shall kill you and eat you. Juicy landlords are my favourite dish.'

The landlord, certain that there was enough work to keep several demons busy for ever, agreed to these terms. He took the demon to a large tank which had been dry for years, and said: 'You must deepen this tank until it is as deep as the height of two palm trees.'

'As you say, master,' said the demon, and set to work.

The landlord went home, feeling sure that the job would take several weeks. His wife gave him a good dinner, and he was just sitting down in his courtyard to enjoy the evening breeze when the demon arrived, casually remarking that the tank was ready.

'The tank ready!' exclaimed the astonished landlord. 'Why, I thought it would take you several weeks! How shall I keep him busy?' he asked, turning to his wife for aid. 'If he goes on at this rate, he'll soon have an excuse for killing and eating me!'

'You must not lose heart, my husband,' said the landlord's wife. 'Get all the work you can out of the demon. You'll never find such a good worker again. And when you have no more work for him, let me know—I'll find something to keep him busy.'

The landlord went out to inspect the tank and found that it had been completed to perfection. Then he set the demon to plough all his farm lands, which extended over a number of villages. This was done in two days. He next asked the demon to dig up all the waste land. This was done in less than a day.

'I'm getting hungry,' said the demon. 'Come on, master, give me more work, quickly!'

The landlord felt helpless. 'My dear friend,' he said, 'my wife says she has a little job for you. Do go and see what it is she wants done. When you have finished, you can come and eat me, because I just can't see how I can keep you busy much longer!'

The landlord's wife, who had been listening to them, now came out of the house, holding in her hands a long hair which she had just pulled out of her head.

'Well, my good demon,' she said. 'I have a very light job for you. I'm sure you will do it in a twinkling. Take this hair, and when you have made it perfectly straight, bring it back to me.'

The demon laughed uproariously, but took the hair and went away with it.

All night he sat in a peepul tree, trying to straighten the hair. He kept rolling it against his thighs and then lifting it up to see if it had become straight. But no, it would still bend! By morning the demon was feeling very tired.

Then he remembered that goldsmiths, when straightening metal wires, would heat them over a fire. So he made a fire and placed the hair over it, and in the twinkling of an eye it frizzled and burnt up.

The demon was horrified. He dared not return to the landlord's wife. Not only had he failed to straighten the hair, but he had lost it too. Feeling that he had disgraced himself, he ran away to another part of the land.

So the landlord was rid of his demon. But he had learnt a lesson. He decided that it was better to have tenants working for him than demons, even if it meant paying for their services.

# The Magic of Tungnath

The mountains and valleys of Garhwal never fail to spring surprises on the traveller in search of the picturesque. It is impossible to know every corner of the Himalayas, which means that there are always new corners to discover; forest or meadow, mountain stream or wayside shrine.

The temple of Tungnath, at a little over 12,000 ft, is the highest shrine on the inner Himalayan range. It lies just below the Chandrashila peak. Some way off the main pilgrim routes it is less frequented than Kedarnath or Badrinath, although it forms a part of the Kedar temple establishment. The priest here is a local man, a Brahmin from the village of Maku; the other Kedar temples have South Indian priests, a tradition begun by Sankaracharya, the eighth century Hindu reformer and revivalist.

Tungnath's lonely eminence gives it a magic of its own. To get there (or beyond it), one passes through some of the most delightful temperate forests in the Garhwal Himalayas. Pilgrim or trekker or just plain rambler, such as myself, one comes away a better man, forest-refreshed and more aware of what the earth was really like before mankind began to strip it bare.

Duiri Tal, a small lake, lies cradled on the hill above Ukhimath at a height of 8,000 ft. It was the favourite spot of one of Garhwal's earliest British Commissioners, J.H. Batten, whose administration continued for twenty years (1836–56). He wrote: 'The day I reached there it was snowing and young trees were laid prostrate under the weight of snow, the lake was frozen over to a depth of about two inches. There was no human habitation, and the place looked a veritable wilderness. The next morning when the sun appeared, the Chaukhamba and many other peaks extending as far as Kedarnath seemed covered with a new quilt of snow as if close at hand. The whole scene was so exquisite that one could not tire of gazing at it for hours. I think a person who has a subdued settled despair in his mind would all of a sudden feel a kind of bounding and exalting cheerfulness which will be imparted to his frame by the atmosphere of Duiri Tal.'

This feeling of uplift can be experienced almost anywhere along the Tungnath range. Duiri Tal is still some way off the beaten track, and anyone wishing to spend the night there should carry a tent; but further along this range, the road ascends to Dugalbeta (at about 9,000 ft) where a PWD rest house, gaily painted, has come up like some exotic orchid in the midst of a lush meadow topped by excelsia pines and pencil cedars. Many an official who has stayed here has rhapsodised on the charms of Dugalbeta; and if you are unofficial (and therefore not entitled to stay in the bungalow), you can move on to Chopta, lusher still, where there is accommodation of a sort for pilgrims and other hardy souls. Two or three little tea-shops provide mattresses and quilts. The Garhwal Mandal Vikas Nigam has put up a rest house. These tourist rest houses, scattered over the length and breadth of Garhwal, are a great boon to travellers; but during the pilgrims season (May/June), they are filled to overflowing, and if you turn up unexpectedly, you might have to take your pick of tea-shop or 'dharamsala', something of a lucky dip, since they vary a good deal in comfort and cleanliness.

The trek from Chopta to Tungnath is only three and a half miles, but in that distance one ascends about 3,000 ft and the pilgrim may be forgiven for feeling that at places he is on a perpendicular path. Like a ladder to heaven, I couldn't help thinking.

In spite of its steepness, my companion, the redoubtable climber Ganesh Saili, insisted that we take a short cut. After clawing our way up tufts of alpine grass, which formed the rungs of our ladder, we were stuck and had to inch our way down again, so that the ascent of Tungnath began to resemble a game of Snakes and Ladders.

A tiny guardian-temple dedicated to Lord Ganesh surprised on top. Nor was I really fatigued; for the cold fresher air and the verdant greenery surrounding us was like an intoxicant. Myriads of wild flowers grew on the open slopes—buttercups, anemones, wild strawberries, forget-me-nots, rock-cross, enough to rival Bhyunders' Valley of Flowers at this time of the year.

But before reaching these alpine meadows, we climb through a rhododendron forest, and here one finds at least three species of this flower: the red-flowering tree rhododendron (found throughout the Himalayas between 6,000 ft and 10,000 ft); a second variety, the Almatta, with flowers that are light red or rosy in colour; and the third, Chimul or white variety, found at heights ranging between 10,000 ft and 13,000 ft. The Chimul is a brushwood, seldom more than twelve feet high and growing slantingly due to the heavy burden of snow it has to carry for almost six months in a year.

The brushwood rhododendrons are the last trees on our ascent, for as we approach Tungnath, the treeline ends and there is nothing between the earth and the sky except grass and rock and tiny flowers. Above us, a couple of crows dive-bomb a hawk, who does his best to escape their attentions. Crows are the world's great survivors. They are capable of living at any height and in any climate; as much at home in the back streets of Delhi as on the heights of Tungnath.

Another surviver, up here at any rate, is the Pika, a sort of mouse-hare, who looks neither like a mouse nor a hare but rather like a tiny guinea-pig; small ears, no tail, grey-brown fur, and chubby feet. They emerge from their holes under the rock to forage for grasses on which to feed. Their simple diet and thick fur enable them to live in extreme cold, and they have been found at 16,000 ft, which is higher than where any mammal lives. The Garhwalis call this little creature the Runda—at any rate, that's what the temple priest called it, adding that it was not averse to entering houses and helping itself to grain and other delicacies. So perhaps there's more in it of mouse than of hare.

These little Rundas were with us all the way from Chopta to Tungnath, peering out from their rocks or scampering about on the hillside, seemingly unconcerned by our presence. At Tungnath they live beneath the temple flagstones. The priest's grandchildren were having a game discovering their burrows; the Rundas would go in at one hole and pop at another; they must have had a system of underground passages.

When we arrived, clouds had gathered over Tungnath, as they do almost every afternoon. The temple looked austere in the gathering gloom.

To some, the name 'tung' indicates 'lofty', from the position of the temple on the highest peak outside the main chain of the Himalayas; others derive it from the word 'tangna'—' to be suspended'—in allusion to the form under which the deity is worshipped here. The form is the Swayambhu Ling; and on Shivratri or the night of Shiva, the true believer may, 'with the eye of faith', see the lingam increase in size; but 'to the evil-minded no such favour is granted'.

The temple, though not very large, is certainly impressive, mainly because of its setting and the solid slabs of grey granite from which it is built. The whole place somehow reminds me of Emily Bronte's Wuthering Heights—bleak, wind-swept, open to the skies. And as you look down from the temple at the little half-deserted hamlet that serves it in summer, the eye is met by grey slate roofs and piles of stones, with just a few hardy souls in residence, for the majority of pilgrims prefer to spend the night down at Chopta.

Even the temple priest, attended by his son and grandsons, complains bitterly of cold. To spend every day barefoot on those cold flagstones must indeed be a hardship. I wince after five minutes of it, made worse by stepping into a puddle of icy water. I shall never make a good pilgrim; no reward for me in this world or the next. But the pandit's feet are literally thick-skinned, and the children seem oblivious to the cold. Still, in October they must be happy to descend to Maku, their home village on the slopes below Dugalbeta.

It begins to rain as we leave the temple. We pass herds of sheep huddled in the ruined dharamsala. The crows are still rushing about the grey weeping skies, although the hawk has very sensibly gone away. A Runda sticks his nose out from his hole, probably to take a look at the weather. There is a clap of thunder and he disappears, like the white rabbit in *Alice in Wonderland*. We are halfway down the Tungnath 'ladder' when it begins to rain quite heavily. And now we pass our first genuine pilgrims, a group of intrepid Bengalis who are heading straight into the storm. They are without umbrellas or raincoats, but they are not to be deterred.

Oaks and rhododendrons flash past as we dash down the steep, winding path. Another short cut, and rock-climber Ganesh Saili takes a tumble, but is cushioned by moss and buttercups. My wristwatch strikes a rock and the glass is shattered. No matter. Time here is of little or no significance. Away with time! Is this, I wonder, the 'bounding and exciting cheerfulness' experienced by Batten and now manifesting itself in me?

The tea-shop beckons. How would one manage in the hills without these wayside tea-shops? Miniature inns, they provide food, shelter, and even lodging to dozens at a time.

We sit on a bench between a Gujar herdsman and a pilgrim who is too feverish to make the climb to the temple. He accepts my offer of an aspirin to go with his tea. We tackle some buns—rock-hard, to match our environment—and wash the pellets down with hot sweet tea.

There is a small shrine here, too, right in front of the tea-shop. It is a slab or rock roughly shaped like a lingam, and it is daubed with vermilion and strewn with offerings of wild flowers. The mica in the rock gives it a beautiful sheen.

I suppose Hinduism comes closest to being a nature religion.

Rivers, rocks, trees, plants, animals and birds, all play their part, both in mythology and in everyday worship. This harmony is most evident in these remote places, where god and mountains co-exist. Tungnath, as yet unspoilt by a materialistic society, exerts its magic on all who come here with open mind and heart.

# Fairy Glen Palace

The old bridle path from Rajpur to Mussoorie passed through Fosterganj at a height of about five thousand feet. In the old days, before the motor road was built, this was the only road to the hill station. You could ride up on a pony, or walk, or be carried in a basket (if you were a child) or in a doolie (if you were a lady or an invalid). The doolie was a cross between a hammock, a stretcher and a sedan chair, if you can imagine such a contraption. It was borne aloft by two perspiring partners. Sometimes they sat down to rest, and dropped you unceremoniously. I have a picture of my grandmother being borne uphill in a doolie, and she looks petrified. There was an incident in which a doolie, its occupant and two bearers, all went over a cliff just before Fosterganj, and perished in the fall. Sometimes you can see the ghost of this poor lady being borne uphill by two phantom bearers.

Fosterganj has its ghosts, of course. And they are something of a distraction.

Writing is my vocation, and I have always tried to follow the apostolic maxim: 'Study to be quiet and to mind your own business.' But in small-town India one is constantly drawn into other people's business, just as they are drawn towards yours. In Fosterganj it was quiet enough, there were few people; there was no excuse for shirking work. But tales of haunted houses and fairy-infested forests have always intrigued me, and when I heard that the ruined palace halfway down to Rajpur was a place to be avoided after dark, it was natural for me to start taking my evening walks in its direction.

Fairy Glen was its name. It had been built on the lines of a Swiss or French chalet, with numerous turrets decorating its many wings—a huge, rambling building, two-storeyed, with numerous balconies and cornices and windows; a hodge-podge of architectural styles, a wedding cake of a palace, built to satisfy the whims and fancies of its late owner, the Raja of Ranipur, a small state near the Nepal border. Maintaining this ornate edifice must have been something of a nightmare; and the present heirs had quite given up on it, for bits of the roof were missing, some windows were without panes, doors had developed cracks and what had once been a garden was now a small jungle. Apparently there was no one living there any more; no sign of a caretaker. I had walked past the wrought-iron gate several times without seeing any signs of life, apart from a large grey cat sunning itself outside a broken window.

Then one evening, walking up from Rajpur, I was caught in a storm.

A wind had sprung up, bringing with it dark, overburdened clouds. Heavy drops of rain were followed by hailstones bouncing off the stony path. Gusts of wind rushed through the oaks, and leaves and small branches were soon swirling through the air. I was still a couple of miles from the Fosterganj bazaar, and I did not fancy sheltering under a tree, as flashes of lightning were beginning to light up the darkening sky. Then I found myself outside the gate of the abandoned palace.

Outside the gate stood an old sentry box. No one had stood

sentry in it for years. It was a good place in which to shelter. But I hesitated because a large bird was perched on the gate, seemingly oblivious to the rain that was still falling.

It looked like a crow or a raven, but it was much bigger than either—in fact, twice the size of a crow, but having all the features of one—and when a flash of lightning lit up the gate, it gave a squawk, opened its enormous wings and took off, flying in the direction of the oak forest. I hadn't seen such a bird before; there was something dark and malevolent and almost supernatural about it. But it had gone, and I darted into the sentry box without further delay.

I had been standing there some ten minutes, wondering when the rain was going to stop, when I heard someone running down the road. As he approached, I could see that he was just a boy, probably eleven or twelve; but in the dark I could not make out his features. He came up to the gate, lifted the latch, and was about to go in when he saw me in the sentry box.

'Kaun? Who are you?' he asked, first in Hindi then in English. He did not appear to be in any way anxious or alarmed.

'Just sheltering from the rain,' I said. 'I live in the bazaar.' He took a small torch from his pocket and shone it in my face.

'Yes, I have seen you there. A tourist.'

'A writer. I stay in places, I don't just pass through.'

'Do you want to come in?'

I hesitated. It was still raining and the roof of the sentry box was leaking badly.

'Do you live here?' I asked.

'Yes, I am the raja's nephew. I live here with my mother. Come in.' He took me by the hand and led me through the gate. His hand was quite rough and heavy for an eleven or twelve-year-old. Instead of walking with me to the front steps and entrance of the old palace, he led me around to the rear of the building, where a faint light glowed in a mullioned window, and in its light I saw that he had a very fresh and pleasant face—a face as yet untouched by the trials of life.

Instead of knocking on the door, he tapped on the window. 'Only strangers knock on the door,' he said. 'When I tap on the window, my mother knows it's me.'

'That's clever of you,' I said.

He tapped again, and the door was opened by an unusually tall woman wearing a kind of loose, flowing gown that looked strange in that place, and on her. The light was behind her, and I couldn't see her face until we had entered the room. When she turned to me, I saw that she had a long reddish scar running down one side of her face. Even so, there was a certain hard beauty in her appearance.

'Make some tea—Mother,' said the boy rather brusquely. 'And something to eat. I'm hungry. Sir, will you have something?' He looked enquiringly at me. The light from a kerosene lamp fell full on his face. He was wide-eyed, full-lipped, smiling; only his voice seemed rather mature for one so young. And he spoke like someone much older, and with an almost unsettling sophistication.

'Sit down, sir.' He led me to a chair, made me comfortable. 'You are not too wet, I hope?'

'No, I took shelter before the rain came down too heavily. But you are wet, you'd better change.'

'It doesn't bother me.' And after a pause, 'Sorry there is no electricity. Bills haven't been paid for years.'

'Is this your place?'

'No, we are only caretakers. Poor relations, you might say. The palace has been in dispute for many years. The raja and his brothers keep fighting over it, and meanwhile it is slowly falling down. The lawyers are happy. Perhaps I should study and become a lawyer some day.'

'Do you go to school?'

'Sometimes.'

'How old are you?'

'Quite old, I'm not sure. Mother, how old am I?' he asked, as the tall woman returned with cups of tea and a plate full of biscuits.

She hesitated, gave him a puzzled look. 'Don't you know? It's on your certificate.'

'I've lost the certificate.'

'No, I've kept it safely.' She looked at him intently, placed a hand on his shoulder, then turned to me and said, 'He is twelve,' with a certain finality.

We finished our tea. It was still raining.

'It will rain all night,' said the boy. 'You had better stay here.'

'It will inconvenience you.'

'No, it won't. There are many rooms. If you do not mind the darkness. Come, I will show you everything. And meanwhile my mother will make some dinner. Very simple food, I hope you won't mind.'

The boy took me around the old palace, if you could still call it that. He led the way with a candle holder from which a large candle threw our exaggerated shadows on the walls.

'What's your name?' I asked, as he led me into what must have been a reception room, still crowded with ornate furniture and bric-a-brac.

'Bhim,' he said. 'But everyone calls me Lucky.'

'And are you lucky?'

He shrugged. 'Don't know...' Then he smiled up at me.

'Maybe you'll bring me luck.'

We walked further into the room. Large oil paintings hung from the walls, gathering mould. Some were portraits of royalty, kings and queens of another era, wearing decorative headgear, strange uniforms, the women wrapped in jewellery—more jewels than garments, it seemed—and sometimes accompanied by children who were also weighed down by excessive clothing. A young man sat on a throne, his lips curled in a sardonic smile.

'My grandfather,' said Bhim.

He led me into a large bedroom taken up by a four-poster bed which had probably seen several royal couples copulating upon it. It looked cold and uninviting, but Bhim produced a voluminous razai from a cupboard and assured me that it would be warm and quite luxurious, as it had been his grandfather's.

'And when did your grandfather die?' I asked.

'Oh, fifty-sixty years ago, it must have been.'

'In this bed, I suppose.'

'No, he was shot accidentally while out hunting. They said it was an accident. But he had enemies.'

'Kings have enemies.... And this was the royal bed?'

He gave me a sly smile; not so innocent after all. 'Many women slept in it. He had many queens.'

'And concubines.'

'What are concubines?'

'Unofficial queens.'

'Yes, those too.'

A worldly-wise boy of twelve.

# The Woman on Platform No. 8

It was my second year at boarding school, and I was sitting on platform no. 8 at Ambala station, waiting for the northern-bound train. I think I was about twelve at the time. My parents considered me old enough to travel alone, and I had arrived by bus at Ambala early in the evening; now there was a wait till midnight before my train arrived. Most of the time I had been pacing up and down the platform, browsing through the bookstall or feeding broken biscuits to stray dogs; trains came and went, the platform would be quiet for a while and then, when a train arrived, it would be an inferno of heaving, shouting, agitated human bodies. As the carriage doors opened, a tide of people would sweep down upon the nervous little ticket collector at the gate; and every time this happened I would be caught in the rush and swept outside the station. Now tired of this game and of ambling about the platform, I sat down on my suitcase and gazed dismally across the railway tracks.

Trolleys rolled past me, and I was conscious of the cries of the various vendors—the men who sold curds and lemon, the sweetmeat seller, the newspaper boy—but I had lost interest in all that was going on along the busy platform, and continued to stare across the railway tracks, feeling bored and a little lonely.

'Are you all alone, my son?' asked a soft voice close behind me.

I looked up and saw a woman standing near me. She was leaning over, and I saw a pale face and dark, kind eyes. She wore no jewels, and was dressed very simply in a white sari.

'Yes, I am going to school,' I said, and stood up respectfully. She seemed poor, but there was a dignity about her that commanded respect.

'I have been watching you for some time,' she said. 'Didn't your parents come to see you off?'

'I don't live here,' I said. 'I had to change trains. Anyway, I can travel alone.'

'I am sure you can,' she said, and I liked her for saying that, and I also liked her for the simplicity of her dress, and for her deep, soft voice and the serenity of her face.

'Tell me, what is your name?' she asked.

'Arun,' I said.

'And how long do you have to wait for your train?'

'About an hour, I think. It comes at twelve o'clock.'

'Then come with me and have something to eat.'

I was going to refuse, out of shyness and suspicion, but she took me by the hand, and then I felt it would be silly to pull my hand away. She told a coolie to look after my suitcase, and then she led me away down the platform. Her hand was gentle, and she held mine neither too firmly nor too lightly. I looked up at her again. She was not young. And she was not old. She must have been over thirty, but had she been fifty, I think she would have looked much the same.

She took me into the station dining room, ordered tea and samosas and jalebis, and at once I began to thaw and take a new interest in this kind woman. The strange encounter had little effect on my appetite. I was a hungry schoolboy, and I ate as much as I could in as polite a manner as possible. She took obvious pleasure in watching me eat, and I think it was the food that strengthened the bond between us and cemented our friendship, for under the influence of the tea and sweets I began to talk quite freely, and told her about my school, my friends, my likes and dislikes. She questioned me quietly from time to time, but preferred listening; she drew me out very well, and I had soon forgotten that we were strangers. But she did not ask me about my family or where I lived, and I did not ask her where she lived. I accepted her for what she had been to me—a quiet, kind and gentle woman who gave sweets to a lonely boy on a railway platform...

After about half an hour we left the dining room and began walking back along the platform. An engine was shunting up and down beside platform no. 8, and as it approached, a boy leapt off the platform and ran across the rails, taking a short cut to the next platform. He was at a safe distance from the engine, but as he leapt across the rails, the woman clutched my arm. Her fingers dug into my flesh, and I winced with pain. I caught her fingers and looked up at her, and I saw a spasm of pain and fear and sadness pass across her face. She watched the boy as he climbed the platform, and it was not until he had disappeared in the crowd that she relaxed her hold on my arm. She smiled at me reassuringly and took my hand again, but her fingers trembled against mine.

'He was all right,' I said, feeling that it was she who needed reassurance.

She smiled gratefully at me and pressed my hand. We walked together in silence until we reached the place where I had left my suitcase. One of my schoolfellows, Satish, a boy of about my age, had turned up with his mother.

'Hello, Arun!' he called. 'The train's coming in late, as usual. Did you know we have a new headmaster this year?'

We shook hands, and then he turned to his mother and said: 'This is Arun, Mother. He is one of my friends, and the best bowler in the class.'

'I am glad to know that,' said his mother, a large imposing woman who wore spectacles. She looked at the woman who held my hand and said: 'And I suppose you're Arun's mother?'

I opened my mouth to make some explanation, but before I could say anything the woman replied: 'Yes, I am Arun's mother.'

I was unable to speak a word. I looked quickly up at the woman, but she did not appear to be at all embarrassed, and was smiling at Satish's mother.

Satish's mother said: 'It's such a nuisance having to wait for the train right in the middle of the night. But one can't let the child wait here alone. Anything can happen to a boy at a big station like this—there are so many suspicious characters hanging about. These days one has to be very careful of strangers.'

'Arun can travel alone, though,' said the woman beside me, and somehow I felt grateful to her for saying that. I had already forgiven her for lying; and besides, I had taken an instinctive dislike to Satish's mother.

'Well, be very careful, Arun,' said Satish's mother looking sternly at me through her spectacles. 'Be very careful when your mother is not with you. And never talk to strangers!'

I looked from Satish's mother to the woman who had given me tea and sweets, and back at Satish's mother.

'I like strangers,' I said.

Satish's mother definitely staggered a little, as obviously she was not used to being contradicted by small boys. 'There you are, you see! If you don't watch over them all the time, they'll walk straight into trouble. Always listen to what your mother tells you,' she said, wagging a fat little finger at me. 'And never, never talk to strangers.'

I glared resentfully at her, and moved closer to the woman who had befriended me. Satish was standing behind his mother, grinning at me, and delighting in my clash with his mother. Apparently he was on my side.

The station bell clanged, and the people who had till now been squatting resignedly on the platform began bustling about.

'Here it comes!' shouted Satish, as the engine whistle shrieked and the front lights played over the rails.

The train moved slowly into the station, the engine hissing and sending out waves of steam. As it came to a stop, Satish jumped on the footboard of a lighted compartment and shouted, 'Come on, Arun, this one's empty!' and I picked up my suitcase and made a dash for the open door.

We placed ourselves at the open windows, and the two women stood outside on the platform, talking up to us. Satish's mother did most of the talking.

'Now don't jump on and off moving trains, as you did just now,' she said. 'And don't stick your heads out of the windows, and don't eat any rubbish on the way.' She allowed me to share the benefit of her advice, as she probably didn't think my 'mother' a very capable person. She handed Satish a bag of fruit, a cricket bat and a big box of chocolates, and told him to share the food with me. Then she stood back from the window to watch how my 'mother' behaved.

I was smarting under the patronizing tone of Satish's mother, who obviously thought mine a very poor family; and

I did not intend giving the other woman away. I let her take my hand in hers, but I could think of nothing to say. I was conscious of Satish's mother staring at us with hard, beady eyes, and I found myself hating her with a firm, unreasoning hate. The guard walked up the platform, blowing his whistle for the train to leave. I looked straight into the eyes of the woman who held my hand, and she smiled in a gentle, understanding way. I leaned out of the window then, and put my lips to her cheek and kissed her.

The carriage jolted forward, and she drew her hand away.

'Goodbye, Mother!' said Satish, as the train began to move slowly out of the station. Satish and his mother waved to each other.

'Goodbye,' I said to the other woman, 'goodbye—Mother…' I didn't wave or shout, but sat still in front of the window, gazing at the woman on the platform. Satish's mother was talking to her, but she didn't appear to be listening; she was looking at me, as the train took me away. She stood there on the busy platform, a pale sweet woman in white, and I watched her until she was lost in the milling crowd.

# A Station for Scandal

Simla, even in the days of Mrs Hauksbee, was never so promiscuous. Simla, after all, was teeming with officials and empire-builders and ambitious young civil servants. If there wasn't room for them in Simla, they went to Nainital, capital of the United Provinces.

But Mussoorie was non-official.

It was not a summer capital. You could live there without feeling that the viceroy or the governor was looking over your shoulder. Those who made their way to Mussoorie did so in order to get as far as possible from viceroys and governors. It was where you went to 'do your own thing', indulge a secret love, or build a cottage for your mistress, far from the stern and censorious eyes of your superior officers. And sometimes the superior officers turned up too, hoping to get away from their junior officer. And if ever the twain met, well, they looked the other way…

Mussoorie is smaller than Simla, all length and no breadth, but from Clouds End in the west to Jabarkhet in the east, it is all of twelve miles, straddling the ridge overlooking the two great rivers, the Ganga and the Jamuna, which are silver slipstreams across the plains below. There is room enough for private lives, for discreet affairs conducted over picnic baskets set down beneath the deodars.

Some years ago I received a letter from a reader in England, wanting to know if there were any Maxwells still living in Mussoorie. He was a Maxwell himself, he said, by his father's first marriage. From what he knew of the family history, there ought to have been several Maxwells by the second marriage, and he wanted to get in touch with them.

He was very frank and mentioned that his father had given up a brilliant career in the Indian Civil Service to marry a fifteen-year-old Muslim girl. He had met the girl in Madras, changed his religion to facilitate the marriage, and then—to avoid 'scandal'—had made his home with her in Mussoorie. His first wife had returned to England with her children.

Although there are no longer any Maxwells in Mussoorie, my neighbour, Miss Bean confirmed that Mr Maxwell's children from his second wife had in fact grown up on the station, each inheriting a considerable property. The old gentleman is buried in the Mussoorie cemetery. The children emigrated, but one granddaughter returned to Mussoorie a few years ago, on a honeymoon with her fourth husband, thus keeping up the family tradition.

Mussoorie, queen of the hills, took this sort of thing in its stride.

The station's reputation was well established as far back as October 1884, when the correspondent of the Calcutta *Statesman* wrote to his paper:

> Last Sunday a sermon was delivered by the Reverend Mr Hackett, belonging to the Church Mission Society; he chose for his text Ezekiel 18th and 2nd verse; the latter clause, 'The fathers have eaten sour grapes and set their children's teeth on edge.' The Reverend gentleman

discoursed upon the 'highly immoral tone of society up
here, that it far surpassed any other hill station in the scale
of morals; that ladies and gentlemen after attending church
proceeded to a drinking shop, a restaurant adjoining the
Library and there indulged freely in *pegs*, not one but
many; that at a fancy Bazaar held this season, a lady stood
up on a chair and offered her kisses to gentlemen at ₹5
each. What would they think of such a state of society at
Home? But this was not all. Married ladies and married
gents formed friendship and associations which tended to
no *good* purpose, and set a bad example.'

The poor Reverend preached to no purpose, and it was perhaps
just as well that he was not alive in the year 1933, when a
lady stood up at a benefit show and auctioned a single kiss for
which a gentleman paid ₹300. (The *Statesman* correspondent
had nothing to say on that occasion; his silence was in itself a
comment on the changing times.)

Mussoorie was probably at its gayest in the '30s. Ballrooms,
skating-rinks and cinema-halls flourished. Beauty salons sprang
up along the Mall. An old advertisement in my possession
announces the superiority of 'Freda' in the art of permanent
waving; she was assisted by Miss Harvey, 'late of "Lucille",
Bedford'.

The war was to change all this; and by the time independence
came to India, most of the European and Anglo-Indian residents
had sold their homes and gone away. Only a few stayed on—
elderly folk like Miss Bean, who had spent her life here, and
others whose meagre incomes did not permit them to go away.

I wonder what brought me back to Mussoorie. True, I had
sometimes been here as a child; and my mother's people had
lived in Dehradun, in the valley below. When I returned to

India, still a young man in my twenties (I had spent only four years in England), I lived in Delhi and Dehra for a few years; and then, without quite knowing why, I found myself visiting the hill station, calling on the oldest resident, Miss Bean, and being told by her that the upper portion of her cottage was to let. On an impulse, I rented it.

Perhaps I really wanted to come back to my beginnings. Because it was in Mussoorie in 1933 (the Year of the Kissing) that my parents first met and enjoyed a typical hill station affair.

I have a photograph of my father and mother, on horseback, riding along the Camel's Back Road not far from the cemetery gate. He was thirty-six then, and had just given up a tea-estate manager's job; she was barely twenty, taking a nurse's training at the Cottage Hospital, just below Gun Hill. A few months later they were husband and wife, living in the heat and dust of Alwar state. I was not born in Mussoorie, but I am pretty sure I had my beginnings there.

There is something in the air of the place—especially in October and November—that is conducive to romance and passion. Miss Bean told me that as a girl she'd had many suitors, and if she did not marry it was more from procrastination than from being passed over. While on all sides elopements and broken marriages were making hill station life exciting, she managed to remain single. She was probably helped in this by her father's reputation for being a very good shot with pistol and Lee-Enfield rifle. She taught elocution in one of the many schools that flourished (and still flourish) in Mussoorie. There is a protective atmosphere about an English public school; an atmosphere which, although it protects one from the outside world, often exposes one to the hazards within the system.

The schools were not without their own scandals. Mrs

Fennimore, the wife of a schoolmaster at Oak Grove, got herself entangled in a defamation suit, each hearing of which grew more and more distasteful to her husband. Unable to stand the whole weary and sordid business, Mr Fennimore hit upon a solution. Loading his revolver, he moved to his wife's bedside and shot her through the head. For no accountable reason he put the weapon under her pillow—obviously no one could have mistaken the death for suicide—and then, going to his study, he leaned over his rifle and shot himself.

Ten years later, in the same school, the headmaster's wife was arrested for attempted murder. She had fired at, and wounded, a junior mistress. The case was later hushed up; the motive remains obscure.

But it was on 25 July 1927, at the height of the season and in the heart of the town, that there took place the double tragedy that set the station agog. It all happened in broad daylight and in a full boarding-house, Zephyr Hall.

Shortly after noon the boarders were startled into brisk activity when a shot rang out from one of the rooms, followed by screams. Other shots followed in quick succession. Those boarders who happened to be in the public rooms or on the verandahs dived for the safety of their own apartments and bolted the doors. One unhappy boarder, however, ignorant of where the man with the gun might be, decided to take no chances and came round a corner with his hands held well above his head—only to run straight into the levelled pistol. Even the man who held it, and who had just shot his own wife, couldn't help laughing.

Mr Owen, the gentleman with the gun, killed his wife, wounded his daughter and finally shot himself. His was the first Christian cremation in Mussoorie, performed in compliance with his wishes expressed long before his dramatic end.

This event had a strange sequel, at least for me.

Last summer, while I was taking a walk along the Mall, I was stopped by a stranger, a small man with pale-blue eyes and thinning hair. He must have been over sixty. Accompanying him was a woman of about thirty, whom he introduced as his wife. He apologized for detaining me, and said, 'But you look as though you have been here for some time. Can you tell me where Miss Garlah lives?'

Miss Garlah, another old resident, is the secretary of the Cemetery Committee, 'house-proud', so to speak, because a visiting representative of the British High Commission once declared that the Mussoorie cemetery was the best-kept 'old' cemetery in North India.

I gave directions to the visitor, and then asked him if he was visiting Mussoorie for the first time. He seemed to welcome the enquiry and showed an eagerness to talk.

'It's nearly fifty years since I was last here,' he said. And he gestured towards the ruins of Zephyr Hall, once the most fashionable boarding-house in the hill station and now occupied by poor squatters and their families. 'That was where we lived for a couple of years. That was where my poor mother died...'

My mind was alive with conjecture and now something seemed to fall into place. 'Not—not Mrs Owen?' I ventured to ask.

'That's right. But surely you're too young to remember.'

'I heard about it,' I lied. Actually, I had a couple of old newspaper clippings on the case.

'My father had a sudden brainstorm. He shot and killed my mother. My sister was badly wounded, but she recovered.'

'And what about you?' I asked. I couldn't remember reading

about a son.

'I was at school in England, just fourteen years old. They'd sent me to England only a few months before it happened. I heard about it much later. Naturally, I couldn't attend my mother's funeral, and I've had to wait fifty years before I could come and see her grave. I know she'd have wanted me to come.'

He took my telephone number and promised to look me up before he left Mussoorie. But I did not see him again. After a few days I began to wonder if I had really met the survivor of a fifty-year-old tragedy, or if he had been just another of the hill station's ghosts. But only a couple of weeks back, when I was walking along the cemetery's lowest terrace looking for a grave that Miss Garlah said needed to be identified (she couldn't manage the steep path down to the bottom terrace), I received confirmation that Mr Owen junior had indeed visited Mussoorie and that he had found his mother's grave.

There before me was the grave of Mrs Owen, victim of her husband's brainstorm. And a new plaque had been set into the stone, with the inscription: 'Mother Dear, I am Here'.

# On Fairy Hill

Those little green lights that I used to see, twinkling away on Pari Tibba—there had to be a scientific explanation for them, I was sure. After dark we see or hear many things that seem mysterious, irrational. And then by the clear light of day we find that the magic, the mystery has an explanation after all.

But I did see those lights occasionally—late at night, when I walked home from town to my little cottage at the edge of the forest. They moved too fast for them to be torches or lanterns carried by people. And as there were no roads on Pari Tibba, they could not have been cycle or cart lamps. Someone told me there was phosphorus in the rocks, and that this probably accounted for the luminous glow emanating from the hillside late at night. Possibly; but I was not convinced.

My encounter with the little people happened by the light of day.

One morning, early in April, purely on an impulse I decided to climb to the top of Pari Tibba and look around for myself. It was springtime in the Himalayan foothills. The sap was rising— in the trees, in the grass, in the wildflowers, in my own veins. I took the path through the oak forest, down to the little steam at the bottom of the hill, and then up the steep slope of Pari

Tibba, hill of the fairies.

It was quite a scramble getting to the top. The path ended at the stream. After that, I had to clutch at brambles and tufts of grass to make the ascent. Fallen pine needles, slippery underfoot, made it difficult to get a foothold. But finally I made it to the top—a grassy plateau fringed by pines and a few wild medlar trees now clothed in white blossom.

It was a pretty spot. And as I was hot and sweaty, I removed most of my clothing and lay down under a medlar to rest. The climb had been quite tiring. But a fresh breeze soon brought me back to life. It made a soft humming sound in the pines. And the grass, sprinkled with yellow buttercups, buzzed with the sound of crickets and grasshoppers.

After some time I stood up and surveyed the scene. To the north, Landour with its rusty red-roofed cottages; to the south, the wide valley and a silver stream flowing towards the Ganga. To the west, rolling hills, patches of forest and a small village tucked into a fold of the mountain.

Disturbed by my presence, a barking deer ran across the clearing and down the opposite slope. A band of long-tailed blue magpies rose from the oak trees, glided across the knoll, and settled in another strand of oaks.

I was alone. Alone with the wind and the sky. It had probably been months, possibly years, since any human had passed that way. The soft lush grass looked most inviting. I lay down again on the sun-warmed sward. Pressed and bruised by my weight, catmint and clover gave out a soft fragrance. A ladybird climbed up my leg and began to explore my body. A swarm of white butterflies fluttered around me.

I slept.

I have no idea how long I slept, but when I awoke it was

to experience an unusual, soothing sensation all over my limbs, as though they were being gently stroked with rose petals.

All lethargy gone, I opened my eyes to find a little girl—or was it a woman?—about two inches high, sitting cross-legged on my chest and studying me intently. Her hair fell in long black tresses. Her skin was the colour of honey. Her firm little breasts were like tiny acorns. She held a buttercup, larger than her hand, and with it she was stroking my tingling flesh.

I was tingling all over. A sensation of sensual joy surged through my limbs.

A tiny boy—or man—completely naked, now joined the elfin girl, and they held hands and looked into my eyes, smiling, their teeth little pearls, their lips soft petals of apricot blossom. Were these the nature spirits, the flower fairies, I had often dreamt of? I raised my head and saw that there were scores of little people all over me—exploring my legs, thighs, waist and arms. Delicate, caring, gentle, caressing creatures. They wanted to love me!

Some of them were laving me with dew or pollen or some soft essence. I closed my eyes. Waves of pure physical pleasure swept over me. I had never known anything like it. My limbs turned to water. The sky revolved around me, and I must have fainted.

When I awoke, perhaps an hour later, the little people had gone. A fragrance of honeysuckle lingered in the air. A deep rumble overhead made me look up. Dark clouds had gathered, threatening rain. Had the thunder frightened them away, to their abode beneath the rocks and tree-roots? Or had they simply tired of sporting with a strange newcomer? Mischievous they were; for when I looked around for my clothes I could not find them anywhere.

A wave of panic surged over me. I ran here and there, looking behind shrubs and tree-trunks, but to no avail. My clothes had disappeared, along with the fairies—if, indeed, they were fairies!

It began to rain. Large drops cannoned off the dry rocks. Then it hailed and soon the slope was covered with ice. There was no shelter. Naked, I ran down the path to the stream. There was no one to see me—only a wild mountain-goat, speeding away in the opposite direction. Gusts of wind slashed rain and hail across my face and body. Panting and shivering, I took shelter beneath an overhanging rock until the storm had passed. By then it was almost dusk and I was able to ascend the path to my cottage without encountering anyone, apart from a band of startled langoors, who chattered excitedly on seeing me.

I couldn't stop shivering, so I went straight to bed. I slept a deep, dreamless sleep and woke up the next morning with a high fever.

Mechanically I dressed, made myself some breakfast and tried to get through the morning's chores. When I took my temperature I found it was a hundred and four. So I swallowed a tablet and went back to bed.

There I lay until late afternoon, when the postman's knocking woke me. I left my letters unopened on my desk (that in itself was unusual) and returned to my bed.

The fever lasted almost a week and left me weak and half-starved. I couldn't have climbed Pari Tibba again, even if I'd wanted to; but I reclined on my window-seat and looked at the clouds drifting over that desolate hill. Desolate it seemed, and yet strangely inhabited. When it grew dark, I waited for those little green fairy lights to appear; but these, it seemed, were now to be denied to me.

And so I returned to my desk, my typewriter, my newspaper articles and correspondence. It was a lonely period in my life. My marriage hadn't worked out: my wife, fond of high society and averse to living with an unsuccessful writer in a remote cottage in the woods, was following her own, more successful career in Mumbai. I had always been rather half-hearted in my approach to making money, whereas she had always wanted more and more of it. She left me—left me with my books and my dreams...

Had it all been a dream, that strange episode on Pari Tibba? Had an over-active imagination conjured up those aerial spirits, those siddhas of the upper air? Or were they underground people, living deep within the bowels of the hill? If I was going to keep my sanity I knew I had better get on with the more mundane aspects of living—such as going into town to buy my groceries, mending the leaking roof, paying the electricity bill, plodding up to the post office and remembering to deposit the odd cheque that came my way. All the mundane things that made life so dull and dreary.

The truth is, what we commonly call life is not life at all. Its routine and settled ways are the curse of life, and we will do almost anything to get away from the trivial, even if it is only for a few hours of forgetfulness in alcohol, drugs, forbidden sex or golf. Some of us would even go underground with the fairies, those little people who have sought refuge in Mother Earth from mankind's killing ways; for they are as vulnerable as butterflies and flowers. All things beautiful are easily destroyed.

I am sitting at my window in the gathering dark, penning these stray thoughts, when I see them coming—hand in hand, walking on a swirl of mist, radiant, suffused with all the colours of the rainbow. For a rainbow has formed a bridge from them, from Pari Tibba, to the edge of my window.

I am ready to go, to love and be loved, in their secret lairs or in the upper air—far from the stifling confines of the world in which we toil...

Come, fairies, carry me away, to love me as you did that summer's day!

# The Night Train at Deoli

When I was at college I used to spend my summer vacations in Dehra, at my grandmother's place. I would leave the plains early in May and return late in July. Deoli was a small station about thirty miles from Dehra. It marked the beginning of the heavy jungles of the Indian Terai.

The train would reach Deoli at about five in the morning when the station would be dimly lit with electric bulbs and oil lamps, and the jungle across the railway tracks would just be visible in the faint light of dawn. Deoli had only one platform, an office for the stationmaster and a waiting room. The platform boasted a tea stall, a fruit vendor and a few stray dogs; not much else because the train stopped there for only ten minutes before rushing on into the forests.

Why it stopped at Deoli, I don't know. Nothing ever happened there. Nobody got off the train and nobody got on. There were never any coolies on the platform. But the train would halt there a full ten minutes and then a bell would sound, the guard would blow his whistle, and presently Deoli would be left behind and forgotten.

I used to wonder what happened in Deoli behind the station walls. I always felt sorry for that lonely little platform and for the place that nobody wanted to visit. I decided that one day

I would get off the train at Deoli and spend the day there just to please the town.

I was eighteen, visiting my grandmother, and the night train stopped at Deoli. A girl came down the platform selling baskets.

It was a cold morning and the girl had a shawl thrown across her shoulders. Her feet were bare and her clothes were old but she was a young girl, walking gracefully and with dignity.

When she came to my window, she stopped. She saw that I was looking at her intently, but at first she pretended not to notice. She had pale skin, set off by shiny black hair and dark, troubled eyes. And then those eyes, searching and eloquent, met mine.

She stood by my window for some time and neither of us said anything. But when she moved on, I found myself leaving my seat and going to the carriage door. I stood waiting on the platform looking the other way. I walked across to the tea stall. A kettle was boiling over on a small fire, but the owner of the stall was busy serving tea somewhere on the train. The girl followed me behind the stall.

'Do you want to buy a basket?' she asked. 'They are very strong, made of the finest cane...'

'No,' I said, 'I don't want a basket.'

We stood looking at each other for what seemed a very long time, and she said, 'Are you sure you don't want a basket?'

'All right, give me one,' I said, and took the one on top and gave her a rupee, hardly daring to touch her fingers.

As she was about to speak, the guard blew his whistle. She said something, but it was lost in the clanging of the bell and the hissing of the engine. I had to run back to my compartment. The carriage shuddered and jolted forward.

I watched her as the platform slipped away. She was alone

on the platform and she did not move, but she was looking at me and smiling. I watched her until the signal box came in the way and then the jungle hid the station. But I could still see her standing there alone...

I stayed awake for the rest of the journey. I could not rid my mind of the picture of the girl's face and her dark, smouldering eyes.

But when I reached Dehra the incident became blurred and distant, for there were other things to occupy my mind. It was only when I was making the return journey, two months later, that I remembered the girl.

I was looking out for her as the train drew into the station, and I felt an unexpected thrill when I saw her walking up the platform. I sprang off the footboard and waved to her.

When she saw me, she smiled. She was pleased that I remembered her. I was pleased that she remembered me. We were both pleased and it was almost like a meeting of old friends.

She did not go down the length of the train selling baskets but came straight to the tea stall. Her dark eyes were suddenly filled with light. We said nothing for some time but we couldn't have been more eloquent.

I felt the impulse to put her on the train there and then, and take her away with me. I could not bear the thought of having to watch her recede into the distance of Deoli station. I took the baskets from her hand and put them down on the ground. She put out her hand for one of them, but I caught her hand and held it.

'I have to go to Delhi,' I said.

She nodded. 'I do not have to go anywhere.'

The guard blew his whistle for the train to leave, and how I hated the guard for doing that.

'I will come again,' I said. 'Will you be here?'

She nodded again and, as she nodded, the bell clanged and the train slid forward. I had to wrench my hand away from the girl and run for the moving train.

This time I did not forget her. She was with me for the remainder of the journey and for long after. All that year she was a bright, living thing. And when the college term finished, I packed in haste and left for Dehra earlier than usual. My grandmother would be pleased at my eagerness to see her.

I was nervous and anxious as the train drew into Deoli, because I was wondering what I should say to the girl and what I should do. I was determined that I wouldn't stand helplessly before her, hardly able to speak or do anything about my feelings.

The train came to Deoli, and I looked up and down the platform but I could not see the girl anywhere.

I opened the door and stepped off the footboard. I was deeply disappointed and overcome by a sense of foreboding. I felt I had to do something and so I ran up to the stationmaster and said, 'Do you know the girl who used to sell baskets here?'

'No, I don't,' said the stationmaster. 'And you'd better get on the train if you don't want to be left behind.'

But I paced up and down the platform and stared over the railings at the station yard. All I saw was a mango tree and a dusty road leading into the jungle. Where did the road go? The train was moving out of the station and I had to run up the platform and jump for the door of my compartment. Then, as the train gathered speed and rushed through the forests, I sat brooding in front of the window.

What could I do about finding a girl I had seen only twice, who had hardly spoken to me, and about whom I knew nothing—absolutely nothing—but for whom I felt a tenderness and responsibility that I had never felt before?

My grandmother was not pleased with my visit after all, because I didn't stay at her place more than a couple of weeks. I felt restless and ill at ease. So I took the train back to the plains, meaning to ask further questions of the stationmaster at Deoli.

But at Deoli there was a new stationmaster. The previous man had been transferred to another post within the past week. The new man didn't know anything about the girl who sold baskets. I found the owner of the tea stall, a small, shrivelled-up man, wearing greasy clothes, and asked him if he knew anything about the girl with the baskets.

'Yes, there was such a girl here. I remember quite well,' he said. 'But she has stopped coming now.'

'Why?' I asked. 'What happened to her?'

'How should I know?' said the man. 'She was nothing to me.'

And once again I had to run for the train.

As Deoli platform receded, I decided that one day I would have to break journey there, spend a day in the town, make inquiries, and find the girl who had stolen my heart with nothing but a look from her dark, impatient eyes.

With this thought I consoled myself throughout my last term in college. I went to Dehra again in the summer and when, in the early hours of the morning, the night train drew into Deoli station, I looked up and down the platform for signs of the girl, knowing I wouldn't find her but hoping just the same.

Somehow, I couldn't bring myself to break journey at Deoli and spend a day there. (If it was all fiction or a film, I reflected, I would have got down and cleaned up the mystery and reached a suitable ending to the whole thing.) I think I was afraid to do this. I was afraid of discovering what really happened to the girl. Perhaps she was no longer in Deoli, perhaps she was married, perhaps she had fallen ill...

In the last few years I have passed through Deoli many times, and I always look out of the carriage window half-expecting to see the same unchanged face smiling up at me. I wonder what happens in Deoli, behind the station walls. But I will never break my journey there. It may spoil my game. I prefer to keep hoping and dreaming and looking out of the window up and down that lonely platform, waiting for the girl with the baskets.

I never break my journey at Deoli but I pass through as often as I can.

# The Wind on Haunted Hill

Whoo, whoo, whoo, cried the wind as it swept down from the Himalayan snows. It hurried over the hills and passes and hummed and moaned through the tall pines and deodars. There was little on Haunted Hill to stop the wind-only a few stunted trees and bushes and the ruins of a small settlement.

On the slopes of the next hill was a village. People kept large stones on their tin roofs to prevent them from being blown off. There was nearly always a strong wind in these parts. Three children were spreading clothes out to dry on a low stone wall, putting a stone on each piece.

Eleven-year-old Usha, dark-haired and rose-cheeked, struggled with her grandfather's long, loose shirt. Her younger brother, Suresh, was doing his best to hold down a bedsheet, while Usha's friend, Binya, a slightly older girl, helped.

Once everything was firmly held down by stones, they climbed up on the flat rocks and sat there sunbathing and staring across the fields at the ruins on Haunted Hill.

'I must go to the bazaar today,' said Usha.

'I wish I could come too,' said Binya. 'But I have to help with the cows.'

'I can come!' said eight-year-old Suresh. He was always ready to visit the bazaar, which was three miles away, on the other side of the hill.

'No, you can't,' said Usha. 'You must help Grandfather chop wood.'

'Won't you feel scared returning alone?' he asked. 'There are ghosts on Haunted Hill!'

'I'll be back before dark. Ghosts don't appear during the day.'

'Are there lots of ghosts in the ruins?' asked Binya.

'Grandfather says so. He says that over a hundred years ago, some Britishers lived on the hill. But the settlement was always being struck by lightning, so they moved away.'

'But if they left, why is the place visited by ghosts?'

'Because, Grandfather says, during a terrible storm, one of the houses was hit by lightning, and everyone in it was killed. Even the children.'

'How many children?'

'Two. A boy and his sister. Grandfather saw them playing there in the moonlight.'

'Wasn't he frightened?'

'No. Old people don't mind ghosts.'

Usha set out for the bazaar at two in the afternoon. It was about an hour's walk. The path went through yellow fields of flowering mustard, then along the saddle of the hill, and up, straight through the ruins. Usha had often gone that way to shop at the bazaar or to see her aunt, who lived in the town nearby.

Wild flowers bloomed on the crumbling walls of the ruins, and a wild plum tree grew straight out of the floor of what had once been a hall. It was covered with soft, white blossoms. Lizards scuttled over the stones, while a whistling thrush, its deep purple plumage glistening in the sunshine, sat on a window-sill and sang its heart out.

Usha sang too, as she skipped lightly along the path, which clipped steeply down to the valley and led to the little town with its quaint bazaar.

Moving leisurely, Usha bought spices, sugar and matches. With the two rupees she had saved from her pocket-money, she chose a necklace of amber-coloured beads for herself and some marbles for Suresh. Then she had her mother's slippers repaired at a cobbler's shop.

Finally, Usha went to visit Aunt Lakshmi at her flat above the shops. They were talking and drinking cups of hot, sweet tea when Usha realized that dark clouds had gathered over the mountains. She quickly picked up her things, said good-bye to her aunt and set out for the village.

Strangely, the wind had dropped. The trees were still, the crickets silent. The crows flew round in circles, then settled in an oak tree.

'I must get home before dark,' thought Usha, hurrying along the path.

But the sky had darkened and a deep rumble echoed over the hills. Usha felt the first heavy drop of rain hit her cheek. Holding the shopping bag close to her body, she quickened her pace until she was almost running. The raindrops were coming down faster now—cold, stinging pellets of rain. A flash of lightning sharply outlined the ruins on the hill, and then all was dark again. Night had fallen.

'I'll have to shelter in the ruins,' Usha thought and began to run. Suddenly the wind sprang up again, but she did not have to fight it. It was behind her now, helping her along, up the steep path and on to the brow of the hill. There was another flash of lightning, followed by a peal of thunder. The ruins loomed before her, grim and forbidding.

Usha remembered part of an old roof that would give some shelter. It would be better than trying to go on. In the dark, with the howling wind, she might stray off the path and fall over the edge of the cliff.

Whoo, whoo, whoo, howled the wind. Usha saw the wild plum tree swaying, its foliage thrashing against the ground. She found her way into the ruins, helped by the constant flicker of lightning. Usha placed her hands flat against a stone wall and moved sideways, hoping to reach the sheltered corner. Suddenly, her hand touched something soft and furry, and she gave a startled cry. Her cry was answered by another—half snarl, half screech—as something leapt away in the darkness.

With a sigh of relief Usha realized that it was the cat that lived in the ruins. For a moment she had been frightened, but now she moved quickly along the wall until she heard the rain drumming on a remnant of a tin roof. Crouched in a corner, she found some shelter. But the tin sheet groaned and clattered as if it would sail away any moment.

Usha remembered that across this empty room stood an old fireplace. Perhaps it would be drier there under the blocked chimney. But she would not attempt to find it just now—she might lose her way altogether.

Her clothes were soaked and water streamed down from her hair, forming a puddle at her feet. She thought she heard a faint cry—the cat again, or an owl? Then the storm blotted out all other sounds.

There had been no time to think of ghosts, but now that she was settled in one place, Usha remembered Grandfather's story about the lightning-blasted ruins. She hoped and prayed that lightning would not strike her.

Thunder boomed over the hills, and the lightning came

quicker now. Then there was a bigger flash, and for a moment the entire ruin was lit up. A streak of blue sizzled along the floor of the building. Usha was staring straight ahead, and, as the opposite wall lit up, she saw, crouching in front of the unused fireplace, two small figures—children!

The ghostly figures seemed to look up and stare back at Usha. And then everything was dark again.

Usha's heart was in her mouth. She had seen without doubt, two ghosts on the other side of the room. She wasn't going to remain in the ruins one minute longer.

She ran towards the big gap in the wall through which she had entered. She was halfway across the open space when something—someone—fell against her. Usha stumbled, got up, and again bumped into something. She gave a frightened scream. Someone else screamed. And then there was a shout, a boy's shout, and Usha instantly recognized the voice.

'Suresh!'

'Usha!'

'Binya!'

They fell into each other's arms, so surprised and relieved that all they could do was laugh and giggle and repeat each other's names.

Then Usha said, 'I thought you were ghosts.'

'We thought you were a ghost,' said Suresh.

'Come back under the roof,' said Usha.

They huddled together in the corner, chattering with excitement and relief.

'When it grew dark, we came looking for you,' said Binya. 'And then the storm broke.'

'Shall we run back together?' asked Usha. 'I don't want to stay here any longer.'

'We'll have to wait,' said Binya. 'The path has fallen away at one place. It won't be safe in the dark, in all this rain.'

'We'll have to wait till morning,' said Suresh, 'and I'm so hungry!'

The storm continued, but they were not afraid now. They gave each other warmth and confidence. Even the ruins did not seem so forbidding.

After an hour the rain stopped, and the thunder grew more distant.

Towards dawn the whistling thrush began to sing. Its sweet, broken notes flooded the ruins with music. As the sky grew lighter, they saw that the plum tree stood upright again, though it had lost all its blossoms.

'Let's go,' said Usha.

Outside the ruins, walking along the brow of the hill, they watched the sky grow pink. When they were some distance away, Usha looked back and said, 'Can you see something behind the wall? It's like a hand waving.'

'It's just the top of the plum tree,' said Binya.

'Good-bye, good-bye...' they heard voices.

'Who said "good-bye"?' asked Usha.

'Not I,' said Suresh.

'Not I,' said Binya.

'I heard someone calling,' said Usha.

'It's only the wind,' assured Binya.

Usha looked back at the ruins. The sun had come up and was touching the top of the wall.

'Come on,' said Suresh. 'I'm hungry.'

They hurried along the path to the village.

'Good-bye, good-bye...' Usha heard them calling. Was it just the wind?

# Panther's Moon

## I

In the entire village, he was the first to get up. Even the dog, a big hill mastiff called Sheroo, was asleep in a corner of the dark room, curled up near the cold embers of the previous night's fire. Bisnu's tousled head emerged from his blanket. He rubbed the sleep from his eyes and sat up on his haunches. Then, gathering his wits, he crawled in the direction of the loud ticking that came from the battered little clock which occupied the second most honoured place in a niche in the wall. The most honoured place belonged to a picture of Ganesha, the god of learning, who had an elephant's head and a fat boy's body.

Bringing his face close to the clock, Bisnu could just make out the hands. It was five o'clock. He had half an hour in which to get ready and leave.

He got up, in vest and underpants, and moved quietly towards the door. The soft tread of his bare feet woke Sheroo, and the big black dog rose silently and padded behind the boy. The door opened and closed, and then the boy and the dog were outside in the early dawn. The month was June, and the nights were warm, even in the Himalayan valleys; but there was fresh dew on the grass. Bisnu felt the dew beneath his feet.

He took a deep breath and began walking down to the stream.

The sound of the stream filled the small valley. At that early hour of the morning, it was the only sound; but Bisnu was hardly conscious of it. It was a sound he lived with and took for granted. It was only when he had crossed the hill, on his way to the town—and the sound of the stream grew distant—that he really began to notice it. And it was only when the stream was too far away to be heard that he really missed its sound.

He slipped out of his underclothes, gazed for a few moments at the goose pimples rising on his flesh, and then dashed into the shallow stream. As he went further in, the cold mountain water reached his loins and navel, and he gasped with shock and pleasure. He drifted slowly with the current, swam across to a small inlet which formed a fairly deep pool, and plunged into the water. Sheroo hated cold water at this early hour. Had the sun been up, he would not have hesitated to join Bisnu. Now he contented himself with sitting on a smooth rock and gazing placidly at the slim brown boy splashing about in the clear water, in the widening light of dawn.

Bisnu did not stay long in the water. There wasn't time. When he returned to the house, he found his mother up, making tea and chapattis. His sister, Puja, was still asleep. She was a little older than Bisnu, a pretty girl with large black eyes, good teeth and strong arms and legs. During the day, she helped her mother in the house and in the fields. She did not go to the school with Bisnu. But when he came home in the evenings, he would try teaching her some of the things he had learnt. Their father was dead. Bisnu, at twelve, considered himself the head of the family.

He ate two chapattis, after spreading butter-oil on them. He drank a glass of hot sweet tea. His mother gave two thick chapattis to Sheroo, and the dog wolfed them down in a few minutes. Then she wrapped two chapattis and a gourd curry in some big green leaves, and handed these to Bisnu. This was his lunch packet. His mother and Puja would take their meal afterwards.

When Bisnu was dressed, he stood with folded hands before the picture of Ganesha. Ganesha is the god who blesses all beginnings. The author who begins to write a new book, the banker who opens a new ledger, the traveller who starts on a journey, all invoke the kindly help of Ganesha. And as Bisnu made a journey every day, he never left without the goodwill of the elephant-headed god.

How, one might ask, did Ganesha get his elephant's head?

When born, he was a beautiful child. Parvati, his mother, was so proud of him that she went about showing him to everyone. Unfortunately she made the mistake of showing the child to that envious planet, Saturn, who promptly burnt off poor Ganesha's head. Parvati in despair went to Brahma, the Creator, for a new head for her son. He had no head to give her, but advised her to search for some man or animal caught in a sinful or wrong act. Parvati wandered about until she came upon an elephant sleeping with its head the wrong way, that is, to the south. She promptly removed the elephant's head and planted it on Ganesha's shoulders, where it took root.

Bisnu knew this story. He had heard it from his mother.

Wearing a white shirt and black shorts, and a pair of worn white keds, he was ready for his long walk to school, five miles up the mountain.

His sister woke up just as he was about to leave. She pushed the hair away from her face and gave Bisnu one of her rare smiles.

'I hope you have not forgotten,' she said.

'Forgotten?' said Bisnu, pretending innocence. 'Is there anything I am supposed to remember?'

'Don't tease me. You promised to buy me a pair of bangles, remember? I hope you won't spend the money on sweets, as you did last time.'

'Oh, yes, your bangles,' said Bisnu. 'Girls have nothing better to do than waste money on trinkets. Now, don't lose your temper! I'll get them for you. Red and gold are the colours you want?'

'Yes, Brother,' said Puja gently, pleased that Bisnu had remembered the colours. 'And for your dinner tonight we'll make you something special. Won't we, Mother?'

'Yes. But hurry up and dress. There is some ploughing to be done today. The rains will soon be here, if the gods are kind.'

'The monsoon will be late this year,' said Bisnu. 'Mr Nautiyal, our teacher, told us so. He said it had nothing to do with the gods.'

'Be off, you are getting late,' said Puja, before Bisnu could begin an argument with his mother. She was diligently winding the old clock. It was quite light in the room. The sun would be up any minute.

Bisnu shouldered his school bag, kissed his mother, pinched his sister's cheeks and left the house. He started climbing the steep path up the mountainside. Sheroo bounded ahead; for he, too, always went with Bisnu to school.

Five miles to school. Every day, except Sunday, Bisnu walked five miles to school; and in the evening, he walked home again. There was no school in his own small village of Manjari, for the village consisted of only five families. The nearest school was at Kemptee, a small township on the bus route through the district of Garhwal. A number of boys walked to school, from distances of two or three miles; their villages were not quite as remote as Manjari. But Bisnu's village lay right at the bottom of the mountain, a drop of over 2,000 feet from Kemptee. There was no proper road between the village and the town.

In Kemptee there was a school, a small mission hospital, a post office and several shops. In Manjari village there were none of these amenities. If you were sick, you stayed at home until you got well; if you were very sick, you walked or were carried to the hospital, up the five mile path. If you wanted to buy something, you went without it; but if you wanted it very badly, you could walk the five miles to Kemptee.

Manjari was known as the Five Mile Village.

Twice a week, if there were any letters, a postman came to the village. Bisnu usually passed the postman on his way to and from school.

There were other boys in Manjari village, but Bisnu was the only one who went to school. His mother would not have fussed if he had stayed at home and worked in the fields. That was what the other boys did; all except lazy Chittru, who preferred fishing in the stream or helping himself to the fruit of other people's trees. But Bisnu went to school. He went because he wanted to. No one could force him to go; and no one could stop him from going. He had set his heart on receiving a good schooling. He wanted to read and write as well as anyone in the big world, the world that seemed to begin only where the mountains ended. He felt cut off from the world in his small valley. He would rather live at the top of a mountain than at the bottom of one. That was why he liked climbing to Kemptee, it took him to the top of the mountain; and from its ridge he could look down on his own valley to the north, and on the wide endless plains stretching towards the south.

The plainsman looks to the hills for the needs of his spirit but the hill man looks to the plains for a living.

Leaving the village and the fields below him, Bisnu climbed steadily up the bare hillside, now dry and brown. By the time the sun was up, he had entered the welcome shade of an oak and rhododendron forest. Sheroo went bounding ahead, chasing squirrels and barking at langoors.

A colony of langoors lived in the oak forest. They fed on oak leaves, acorns and other green things, and usually remained in the trees, coming down to the ground only to play or bask in the sun. They were beautiful, supple-limbed animals, with black faces and silver-grey coats and long, sensitive tails. They leapt from tree to tree with great agility. The young ones wrestled on the grass like boys.

A dignified community, the langoors did not have the cheekiness or dishonest habits of the red monkeys of the plains; they did not approach dogs or humans. But they had grown used to Bisnu's comings and goings, and did not fear him. Some of the older ones would watch him quietly, a little puzzled. They did not go near the town, because the Kemptee boys threw stones at them. And anyway, the oak forest gave them all the food they required.

Emerging from the trees, Bisnu crossed a small brook. Here he stopped to drink the fresh clean water of a spring. The brook tumbled down the mountain and joined the river a little below Bisnu's village. Coming from another direction was a second path, and at the junction of the two paths Sarru was waiting for him.

Sarru came from a small village about three miles from Bisnu's and closer to the town. He had two large milk cans slung over his shoulders. Every morning he carried this milk to town, selling one can to the school and the other to Mrs Taylor, the lady doctor at the small mission hospital. He was a little older than Bisnu but not as well-built.

They hailed each other, and Sarru fell into step beside Bisnu. They often met at this spot, keeping each other company for the remaining two miles to Kemptee.

'There was a panther in our village last night,' said Sarru.

This information interested but did not excite Bisnu. Panthers were common enough in the hills and did not usually present a problem except during the winter months, when their natural prey was scarce. Then, occasionally, a panther would take to haunting the outskirts of a village, seizing a careless dog or a stray goat.

'Did you lose any animals?' asked Bisnu.

'No. It tried to get into the cowshed but the dogs set up an alarm. We drove it off.'

'It must be the same one which came around last winter. We lost a calf and two dogs in our village.'

'Wasn't that the one the shikaris wounded? I hope it hasn't become a cattle lifter.'

'It could be the same. It has a bullet in its leg. These hunters are the people who cause all the trouble. They think it's easy to shoot a panther. It would be better if they missed altogether, but they usually wound it.'

'And then the panther's too slow to catch the barking deer, and starts on our own animals.'

'We're lucky it didn't become a man-eater. Do you remember the man-eater six years ago? I was very small then. My father told me all about it. Ten people were killed in our valley alone. What happened to it?'

'I don't know. Some say it poisoned itself when it ate the headman of another village.'

Bisnu laughed. 'No one liked that old villain. He must have been a man-eater himself in some previous existence!' They linked arms and scrambled up the stony path. Sheroo began barking and ran ahead. Someone was coming down the path.

It was Mela Ram, the postman.

## II

'Any letters for us?' asked Bisnu and Sarru together.

They never received any letters but that did not stop them from asking. It was one way of finding out who had received letters.

'You're welcome to all of them,' said Mela Ram, 'if you'll carry my bag for me.'

'Not today,' said Sarru. 'We're busy today. Is there a letter from Corporal Ghanshyam for his family?'

'Yes, there is a postcard for his people. He is posted on the Ladakh border now and finds it very cold there.'

Postcards, unlike sealed letters, were considered public property and were read by everyone. The senders knew that too, and so Corporal Ghanshyam Singh was careful to mention that he expected a promotion very soon. He wanted everyone in his village to know it.

Mela Ram, complaining of sore feet, continued on his way, and the boys carried on up the path. It was eight o'clock when they reached Kemptee. Dr Taylor's outpatients were just beginning to trickle in at the hospital gate. The doctor was trying to prop up a rose creeper which had blown down during the night. She liked attending to her plants in the mornings, before starting on her patients. She found this helped her in her work. There was a lot in common between ailing plants and ailing people.

Dr Taylor was fifty, white-haired but fresh in the face and full of vitality. She had been in India for twenty years, and ten of these had been spent working in the hill regions.

She saw Bisnu coming down the road. She knew about the boy and his long walk to school and admired him for his keenness and sense of purpose. She wished there were more like him.

Bisnu greeted her shyly. Sheroo barked and put his paws up on the gate.

'Yes, there's a bone for you,' said Dr Taylor. She often put aside bones for the big black dog, for she knew that Bisnu's people could not afford to give the dog a regular diet of meat—though he did well enough on milk and chapattis.

She threw the bone over the gate and Sheroo caught it before it fell. The school bell began ringing and Bisnu broke into a run. Sheroo loped along behind the boy.

When Bisnu entered the school gate, Sheroo sat down on the grass of the compound. He would remain there until the lunchbreak. He knew of various ways of amusing himself during school hours and had friends among the bazaar dogs. But just then he didn't want company. He had his bone to get on with.

Mr Nautiyal, Bisnu's teacher, was in a bad mood. He was a keen rose grower and only that morning, on getting up and looking out of his bedroom window, he had been horrified to see a herd of goats in his garden. He had chased them down the road with a stick but the damage had already been done. His prize roses had all been consumed.

Mr Nautiyal had been so upset that he had gone without his breakfast. He had also cut himself whilst shaving. Thus, his mood had gone from bad to worse. Several times during the day, he brought down his ruler on the knuckles of any boy who irritated him. Bisnu was one of his best pupils. But even Bisnu irritated him by asking too many questions about a new sum which Mr Nautiyal didn't feel like explaining.

That was the kind of day it was for Mr Nautiyal. Most schoolteachers know similar days.

'Poor Mr Nautiyal,' thought Bisnu. 'I wonder why he's so upset. It must be because of his pay. He doesn't get much money. But he's a good teacher. I hope he doesn't take another job.'

But after Mr Nautiyal had eaten his lunch, his mood improved (as it always did after a meal), and the rest of the day passed serenely. Armed with a bundle of homework, Bisnu came out from the school compound at four o'clock, and was immediately joined by Sheroo. He proceeded down the road in the company of several of his classfellows. But he did not linger long in the bazaar. There were five miles to walk, and he did not like to get home too late. Usually, he reached his house just as it was beginning to get dark. Sarru had gone home long ago, and Bisnu had to make the return journey on his own. It was a good opportunity to memorize the words of an English poem he had been asked to learn.

Bisnu had reached the little brook when he remembered the bangles he had promised to buy for his sister.

'Oh, I've forgotten them again,' he said aloud. 'Now I'll catch it—and she's probably made something special for my dinner!'

Sheroo, to whom these words were addressed, paid no attention but bounded off into the oak forest. Bisnu looked around for the monkeys but they were nowhere to be seen.

'Strange,' he thought, 'I wonder why they have disappeared.' He was startled by a sudden sharp cry, followed by a fierce yelp. He knew at once that Sheroo was in trouble. The noise came from the bushes down the khud, into which the dog had rushed but a few seconds previously.

Bisnu jumped off the path and ran down the slope towards the bushes. There was no dog and not a sound. He whistled and called, but there was no response. Then he saw something lying on the dry grass. He picked it up. It was a portion of a dog's collar, stained with blood. It was Sheroo's collar and Sheroo's blood.

Bisnu did not search further. He knew, without a doubt, that Sheroo had been seized by a panther. No other animal could have attacked so silently and swiftly and carried off a big dog without a struggle. Sheroo was dead—must have been dead within seconds of being caught and flung into the air. Bisnu knew the danger that lay in wait for him if he followed the blood trail through the trees. The panther would attack anyone who interfered with its meal. With tears starting in his eyes, Bisnu carried on down the path to the village. His fingers still clutched the little bit of bloodstained collar that was all that was left to him of his dog.

### III

Bisnu was not a very sentimental boy, but he sorrowed for his dog who had been his companion on many a hike into the hills and forests. He did not sleep that night, but turned restlessly from side to side moaning softly. After some time he felt Puja's hand on his head. She began stroking his brow. He took her hand in his own and the clasp of her rough, warm familiar hand gave him a feeling of comfort and security.

Next morning, when he went down to the stream to bathe, he missed the presence of his dog. He did not stay long in the water. It wasn't as much fun when there was no Sheroo to watch him.

When Bisnu's mother gave him his food, she told him to be careful and hurry home that evening. A panther, even if it is only a cowardly lifter of sheep or dogs, is not to be trifled with. And this particular panther had shown some daring by seizing the dog even before it was dark.

Still, there was no question of staying away from school. If Bisnu remained at home every time a panther put in an appearance, he might just as well stop going to school altogether.

He set off even earlier than usual and reached the meeting of the paths long before Sarru. He did not wait for his friend, because he did not feel like talking about the loss of his dog. It was not the day for the postman, and so Bisnu reached Kemptee without meeting anyone on the way. He tried creeping past the hospital gate unnoticed, but Dr Taylor saw him and the first thing she said was: 'Where's Sheroo? I've got something for him.'

When Dr Taylor saw the boy's face, she knew at once that something was wrong.

'What is it, Bisnu?' she asked. She looked quickly up and down the road. 'Is it Sheroo?'

He nodded gravely.

'A panther took him,' he said.

'In the village?'

'No, while we were walking home through the forest. I did not see anything—but I heard.'

Dr Taylor knew that there was nothing she could say that would console him, and she tried to conceal the bone which she had brought out for the dog, but Bisnu noticed her hiding it behind her back and the tears welled up in his eyes. He turned away and began running down the road.

His schoolfellows noticed Sheroo's absence and questioned Bisnu. He had to tell them everything. They were full of sympathy, but they were also quite thrilled at what had happened and kept pestering Bisnu for all the details. There was a lot of noise in the classroom, and Mr Nautiyal had to call for order. When he learnt what had happened, he patted Bisnu on the head and told him that he need not attend school for the rest of the day. But Bisnu did not want to go home. After school, he got into a fight with one of the boys, and that helped him forget.

<h2 style="text-align:center">IV</h2>

The panther that plunged the village into an atmosphere of gloom and terror may not have been the same panther that took Sheroo. There was no way of knowing, and it would have made no difference, because the panther that came by night and struck at the people of Manjari was that most feared of wild creatures, a man-eater.

Nine-year-old Sanjay, son of Kalam Singh, was the first child to be attacked by the panther.

Kalam Singh's house was the last in the village and nearest the stream. Like the other houses, it was quite small, just a room above and a stable below, with steps leading up from outside the house. He lived there with his wife, two sons (Sanjay was the youngest) and little daughter Basanti who had just turned three.

Sanjay had brought his father's cows home after grazing them on the hillside in the company of other children. He had also brought home an edible wild plant, which his mother cooked into a tasty dish for their evening meal. They had their food at dusk, sitting on the floor of their single room, and soon after settled down for the night. Sanjay curled up in his favourite spot, with his head near the door, where he got a little fresh air. As the nights were warm, the door was usually left a little ajar. Sanjay's mother piled ash on the embers of the fire and the family was soon asleep.

No one heard the stealthy padding of a panther approaching the door, pushing it wide open. But suddenly there were sounds of a frantic struggle, and Sanjay's stifled cries were mixed with the grunts of the panther. Kalam Singh leapt to his feet with a shout. The panther had dragged Sanjay out of the door and was pulling him down the steps, when Kalam Singh started battering at the animal with a large stone. The rest of the family screamed in terror, rousing the entire village. A number of men came to Kalam Singh's assistance, and the panther was driven off. But Sanjay lay unconscious.

Someone brought a lantern and the boy's mother screamed when she saw her small son with his head lying in a pool of blood. It looked as if the side of his head had been eaten off by the panther. But he was still alive, and as Kalam Singh plastered ash on the boy's head to stop the bleeding, he found that though the scalp had been torn off one side of the head, the bare bone was smooth and unbroken.

'He won't live through the night,' said a neighbour. 'We'll have to carry him down to the river in the morning.'

The dead were always cremated on the banks of a small river which flowed past Manjari village.

Suddenly the panther, still prowling about the village, called out in rage and frustration, and the villagers rushed to their homes in panic and barricaded themselves in for the night.

Sanjay's mother sat by the boy for the rest of the night, weeping and watching. Towards dawn he started to moan and show signs of coming round. At this sign of returning consciousness, Kalam Singh rose determinedly and looked around for his stick.

He told his elder son to remain behind with the mother and daughter, as he was going to take Sanjay to Dr Taylor at the hospital.

'See, he is moaning and in pain,' said Kalam Singh. 'That means he has a chance to live if he can be treated at once.'

With a stout stick in his hand, and Sanjay on his back, Kalam Singh set off on the two miles of hard mountain track to the hospital at Kemptee. His son, a bloodstained cloth around his head, was moaning but still unconscious. When at last Kalam Singh climbed up through the last fields below the hospital, he asked for the doctor and stammered out an account of what had happened.

It was a terrible injury, as Dr Taylor discovered. The bone over almost one-third of the head was bare and the scalp was torn all round. As the father told his story, the doctor cleaned and dressed the wound, and then gave Sanjay a shot of penicillin to prevent sepsis. Later, Kalam Singh carried the boy home again.

## V

After this, the panther went away for some time. But the people of Manjari could not be sure of its whereabouts. They kept to their houses after dark and shut their doors. Bisnu had to stop going to school, because there was no one to accompany him and it was dangerous to go alone. This worried him, because his final exam was only a few weeks off and he would be missing important classwork. When he wasn't in the fields, helping with the sowing of rice and maize, he would be sitting in the shade of a chestnut tree, going through his well-thumbed second-hand school books. He had no other reading, except for a copy of the Ramayana and a Hindi translation of *Alice in Wonderland*. These were well-preserved, read only in fits and starts, and usually kept locked in his mother's old tin trunk.

Sanjay had nightmares for several nights and woke up screaming. But with the resilience of youth, he quickly recovered. At the end of the week he was able to walk to the hospital, though his father always accompanied him. Even a desperate panther will hesitate to attack a party of two. Sanjay, with his thin little face and huge bandaged head, looked a pathetic figure, but he was getting better and the wound looked healthy.

Bisnu often went to see him, and the two boys spent long hours together near the stream. Sometimes Chittru would join them, and they would try catching fish with a home-made net. They were often successful in taking home one or two mountain trout. Sometimes, Bisnu and Chittru wrestled in the shallow water or on the grassy banks of the stream. Chittru was a chubby boy with a broad chest, strong legs and thighs, and when he used his weight he got Bisnu under him. But Bisnu was hard and wiry and had very strong wrists and fingers. When he had Chittru in a vice, the bigger boy would cry out and give up the struggle. Sanjay could not join in these games.

He had never been a very strong boy and he needed plenty of rest if his wounds were to heal well.

The panther had not been seen for over a week, and the people of Manjari were beginning to hope that it might have moved on over the mountain or further down the valley.

'I think I can start going to school again,' said Bisnu. 'The panther has gone away.'

'Don't be too sure,' said Puja. 'The moon is full these days and perhaps it is only being cautious.'

'Wait a few days,' said their mother. 'It is better to wait.

Perhaps you could go the day after tomorrow when Sanjay goes to the hospital with his father. Then you will not be alone.'

And so, two days later, Bisnu went up to Kemptee with Sanjay and Kalam Singh. Sanjay's wound had almost healed over. Little islets of flesh had grown over the bone. Dr Taylor told him that he need come to see her only once a fortnight, instead of every third day.

Bisnu went to his school, and was given a warm welcome by his friends and by Mr Nautiyal.

'You'll have to work hard,' said his teacher. 'You have to catch up with the others. If you like, I can give you some extra time after classes.'

'Thank you, sir, but it will make me late,' said Bisnu. 'I must get home before it is dark, otherwise my mother will worry. I think the panther has gone but nothing is certain.'

'Well, you mustn't take risks. Do your best, Bisnu. Work hard and you'll soon catch up with your lessons.'

Sanjay and Kalam Singh were waiting for him outside the school. Together they took the path down to Manjari, passing the postman on the way. Mela Ram said he had heard that the panther was in another district and that there was nothing to fear. He was on his rounds again.

Nothing happened on the way. The langoors were back in their favourite part of the forest. Bisnu got home just as the kerosene lamp was being lit. Puja met him at the door with a winsome smile.

'Did you get the bangles?' she asked.

But Bisnu had forgotten again.

## VI

There had been a thunderstorm and some rain—a short, sharp shower which gave the villagers hope that the monsoon would arrive on time. It brought out the thunder lilies—pink, crocus-like flowers which sprang up on the hillsides immediately after a summer shower.

Bisnu, on his way home from school, was caught in the rain. He knew the shower would not last, so he took shelter in a small cave and, to pass the time, began doing sums, scratching figures in the damp earth with the end of a stick.

When the rain stopped, he came out from the cave and continued down the path. He wasn't in a hurry. The rain had made everything smell fresh and good. The scent from fallen pine needles rose from wet earth. The leaves of the oak trees had been washed clean and a light breeze turned them about, showing their silver undersides. The birds, refreshed and high-spirited, set up a terrific noise. The worst offenders were the yellow-bottomed bulbuls who squabbled and fought in the blackberry bushes. A barbet, high up in the branches of a deodar, set up its querulous, plaintive call. And a flock of bright green parrots came swooping down the hill to settle in a wild plum tree and feast on the unripe fruit. The langoors, too, had been revived by the rain. They leapt friskily from tree to tree greeting Bisnu with little grunts.

He was almost out of the oak forest when he heard a faint bleating. Presently, a little goat came stumbling up the path towards him. The kid was far from home and must have strayed from the rest of the herd. But it was not yet conscious of being lost. It came to Bisnu with a hop, skip and a jump and started nuzzling against his legs like a cat.

'I wonder who you belong to,' mused Bisnu, stroking the

little creature. 'You'd better come home with me until someone claims you.'

He didn't have to take the kid in his arms. It was used to humans and followed close at his heels. Now that darkness was coming on, Bisnu walked a little faster.

He had not gone very far when he heard the sawing grunt of a panther.

The sound came from the hill to the right, and Bisnu judged the distance to be anything from a hundred to two hundred yards. He hesitated on the path, wondering what to do. Then he picked the kid up in his arms and hurried on in the direction of home and safety.

The panther called again, much closer now. If it was an ordinary panther, it would go away on finding that the kid was with Bisnu. If it was the man-eater, it would not hesitate to attack the boy, for no man-eater fears a human. There was no time to lose and there did not seem much point in running. Bisnu looked up and down the hillside. The forest was far behind him and there were only a few trees in his vicinity. He chose a spruce.

The branches of the Himalayan spruce are very brittle and snap easily beneath a heavy weight. They were strong enough to support Bisnu's light frame. It was unlikely they would take the weight of a full-grown panther. At least that was what Bisnu hoped.

Holding the kid with one arm, Bisnu gripped a low branch and swung himself up into the tree. He was a good climber. Slowly but confidently he climbed halfway up the tree, until he was about twelve feet above the ground. He couldn't go any higher without risking a fall.

He had barely settled himself in the crook of a branch when

the panther came into the open, running into the clearing at a brisk trot. This was no stealthy approach, no wary stalking of its prey. It was the man-eater, all right. Bisnu felt a cold shiver run down his spine. He felt a little sick.

The panther stood in the clearing with a slight thrusting forward of the head. This gave it the appearance of gazing intently and rather short-sightedly at some invisible object in the clearing. But there is nothing short-sighted about a panther's vision. Its sight and hearing are acute.

Bisnu remained motionless in the tree and sent up a prayer to all the gods he could think of. But the kid began bleating. The panther looked up and gave its deep-throated, rasping grunt—a fearsome sound, calculated to strike terror in any treeborne animal. Many a monkey, petrified by a panther's roar, has fallen from its perch to make a meal for Mr Spots. The man-eater was trying the same technique on Bisnu. But though the boy was trembling with fright, he clung firmly to the base of the spruce tree.

The panther did not make any attempt to leap into the tree. Perhaps, it knew instinctively that this was not the type of tree that it could climb. Instead, it described a semicircle round the tree, keeping its face turned towards Bisnu. Then it disappeared into the bushes.

The man-eater was cunning. It hoped to put the boy off his guard, perhaps entice him down from the tree. For, a few seconds later, with a half-humorous growl, it rushed back into the clearing and then stopped, staring up at the boy in some surprise. The panther was getting frustrated. It snarled, and putting its forefeet up against the tree trunk began scratching at the bark in the manner of an ordinary domestic cat. The tree shook at each thud of the beast's paw.

Bisnu began shouting for help.

The moon had not yet come up. Down in Manjari village, Bisnu's mother and sister stood in their lighted doorway, gazing anxiously up the pathway. Every now and then, Puja would turn to take a look at the small clock.

Sanjay's father appeared in a field below. He had a kerosene lantern in his hand.

'Sister, isn't your boy home as yet?' he asked.

'No, he hasn't arrived. We are very worried. He should have been home an hour ago. Do you think the panther will be about tonight? There's going to be a moon.'

'True, but it will be dark for another hour. I will fetch the other menfolk, and we will go up the mountain for your boy. There may have been a landslide during the rain. Perhaps the path has been washed away.'

'Thank you, brother. But arm yourselves, just in case the panther is about.'

'I will take my spear,' said Kalam Singh. 'I have sworn to spear that devil when I find him. There is some evil spirit dwelling in the beast and it must be destroyed!'

'I am coming with you,' said Puja.

'No, you cannot go,' said her mother. 'It's bad enough that Bisnu is in danger. You stay at home with me. This is work for men.'

'I shall be safe with them,' insisted Puja. 'I am going, Mother!' And she jumped down the embankment into the field and followed Sanjay's father through the village.

Ten minutes later, two men armed with axes had joined Kalam Singh in the courtyard of his house, and the small party moved silently and swiftly up the mountain path. Puja walked in the middle of the group, holding the lantern. As soon as the village lights were hidden by a shoulder of the hill, the men began to shout—both to frighten the panther, if it was about, and to give themselves courage.

Bisnu's mother closed the front door and turned to the image of Ganesha, the god, for comfort and help.

Bisnu's calls were carried on the wind, and Puja and the men heard him while they were still half a mile away. Their own shouts increased in volume and, hearing their voices, Bisnu felt strength return to his shaking limbs. Emboldened by the approach of his own people, he began shouting insults at the snarling panther, then throwing twigs and small branches at the enraged animal. The kid added its bleats to the boy's shouts, the birds took up the chorus. The langoors squealed and grunted, the searchers shouted themselves hoarse, and the panther howled with rage. The forest had never before been so noisy.

As the search party drew near, they could hear the panther's savage snarls, and hurried, fearing that perhaps Bisnu had been seized. Puja began to run.

'Don't rush ahead, girl,' said Kalam Singh. 'Stay between us.'

The panther, now aware of the approaching humans, stood still in the middle of the clearing, head thrust forward in a familiar stance. There seemed too many men for one panther. When the animal saw the light of the lantern dancing between the trees, it turned, snarled defiance and hate, and without another look at the boy in the tree, disappeared into the bushes. It was not yet ready for a showdown.

## VII

Nobody turned up to claim the little goat, so Bisnu kept it. A goat was a poor substitute for a dog, but, like Mary's lamb, it followed Bisnu wherever he went, and the boy couldn't help being touched by its devotion. He took it down to the stream, where it would skip about in the shallows and nibble the sweet grass that grew on the banks.

As for the panther, frustrated in its attempt on Bisnu's life, it did not wait long before attacking another human.

It was Chittru who came running down the path one afternoon, bubbling excitedly about the panther and the postman.

Chittru, deeming it safe to gather ripe bilberries in the daytime, had walked about half a mile up the path from the village, when he had stumbled across Mela Ram's mailbag lying on the ground. Of the postman himself there was no sign. But a trail of blood led through the bushes.

Once again, a party of men headed by Kalam Singh and accompanied by Bisnu and Chittru, went out to look for the postman. But though they found Mela Ram's bloodstained clothes, they could not find his body. The panther had made no mistake this time.

It was to be several weeks before Manjari had a new postman.

A few days after Mela Ram's disappearance, an old woman was sleeping with her head near the open door of her house. She had been advised to sleep inside with the door closed, but the nights were hot and anyway the old woman was a little deaf, and in the middle of the night, an hour before moonrise, the panther seized her by the throat. Her strangled cry woke her grown-up son, and all the men in the village woke up at his shouts and came running.

The panther dragged the old woman out of the house and down the steps, but left her when the men approached with their axes and spears, and made off into the bushes. The old woman was still alive, and the men made a rough stretcher of bamboo and vines and started carrying her up the path. But they had not gone far when she began to cough, and because of her terrible throat wounds, her lungs collapsed and she died.

It was the 'dark of the month'—the week of the new moon when nights are darkest.

Bisnu, closing the front door and lighting the kerosene lantern, said, 'I wonder where that panther is tonight!'

The panther was busy in another village: Sarru's village.

A woman and her daughter had been out in the evening bedding the cattle down in the stable. The girl had gone into the house and the woman was following. As she bent down to go in at the low door, the panther sprang from the bushes. Fortunately, one of its paws hit the doorpost and broke the force of the attack, or the woman would have been killed. When she cried out, the men came round shouting and the panther slunk off. The woman had deep scratches on her back and was badly shocked.

The next day, a small party of villagers presented themselves in front of the magistrate's office at Kemptee and demanded that something be done about the panther. But the magistrate was away on tour, and there was no one else in Kemptee who had a gun. Mr Nautiyal met the villagers and promised to write to a well-known shikari, but said that it would be at least a fortnight before the shikari would be able to come.

Bisnu was fretting because he could not go to school. Most boys would be only too happy to miss school, but when you are living in a remote village in the mountains and having an education is the only way of seeing the world, you look forward to going to school, even if it is five miles from home. Bisnu's exams were only two weeks off, and he didn't want to remain in the same class while the others were promoted. Besides, he knew he could pass even though he had missed a number of lessons. But he had to sit for the exams. He couldn't miss them.

'Cheer up, Bhaiya,' said Puja, as they sat drinking glasses of hot tea after their evening meal. 'The panther may go away once the rains break.'

'Even the rains are late this year,' said Bisnu. 'It's so hot and dry. Can't we open the door?'

'And be dragged down the steps by the panther?' said his mother. 'It isn't safe to have the window open, let alone the door.' And she went to the small window—through which a cat would have found difficulty in passing—and bolted it firmly.

With a sigh of resignation, Bisnu threw off all his clothes except his underwear and stretched himself out on the earthen floor.

'We will be rid of the beast soon,' said his mother. 'I know it in my heart. Our prayers will be heard, and you shall go to school and pass your exams.'

To cheer up her children, she told them a humorous story which had been handed down to her by her grandmother. It was all about a tiger, a panther and a bear, the three of whom were made to feel very foolish by a thief hiding in the hollow trunk of a banyan tree. Bisnu was sleepy and did not listen very attentively. He dropped off to sleep before the story was finished.

When he woke, it was dark and his mother and sister were asleep on the cot. He wondered what it was that had woken him. He could hear his sister's easy breathing and the steady ticking of the clock. Far away an owl hooted—an unlucky sign, his mother would have said; but she was asleep and Bisnu was not superstitious.

And then he heard something scratching at the door, and

the hair on his head felt tight and prickly. It was like a cat scratching, only louder. The door creaked a little whenever it felt the impact of the paw—a heavy paw, as Bisnu could tell from the dull sound it made.

'It's the panther,' he muttered under his breath, sitting up on the hard floor.

The door, he felt, was strong enough to resist the panther's weight. And if he set up an alarm, he could rouse the village. But the middle of the night was no time for the bravest of men to tackle a panther.

In a corner of the room stood a long bamboo stick with a sharp knife tied to one end, which Bisnu sometimes used for spearing fish. Crawling on all fours across the room, he grasped the home-made spear, and then scrambling on to a cupboard, he drew level with the skylight window. He could get his head and shoulders through the window.

'What are you doing up there?' said Puja, who had woken up at the sound of Bisnu shuffling about the room.

'Be quiet,' said Bisnu. 'You'll wake Mother.'

Their mother was awake by now. 'Come down from there, Bisnu. I can hear a noise outside.'

'Don't worry,' said Bisnu, who found himself looking down on the wriggling animal which was trying to get its paw in under the door. With his mother and Puja awake, there was no time to lose. He had got the spear through the window, and though he could not manoeuvre it so as to strike the panther's head, he brought the sharp end down with considerable force on the animal's rump.

With a roar of pain and rage the man-eater leapt down from the steps and disappeared into the darkness. It did not pause to see what had struck it. Certain that no human could have come upon it in that fashion, it ran fearfully to its lair, howling until the pain subsided.

## VIII

A panther is an enigma. There are occasions when it proves himself to be the most cunning animal under the sun, and yet the very next day it will walk into an obvious trap that no self-respecting jackal would ever go near. One day a panther will prove itself to be a complete coward and run like a hare from a couple of dogs, and the very next it will dash in amongst half a dozen men sitting round a camp fire and inflict terrible injuries on them.

It is not often that a panther is taken by surprise, as its power of sight and hearing are very acute. It is a master at the art of camouflage, and its spotted coat is admirably suited for the purpose. It does not need heavy jungle to hide in. A couple of bushes and the light and shade from surrounding trees are enough to make it almost invisible.

Because the Manjari panther had been fooled by Bisnu, it did not mean that it was a stupid panther. It simply meant that it had been a little careless. And Bisnu and Puja, growing in confidence since their midnight encounter with the animal, became a little careless themselves.

Puja was hoeing the last field above the house and Bisnu, at the other end of the same field, was chopping up several branches of green oak, prior to leaving the wood to dry in the loft. It was late afternoon and the descending sun glinted in patches on the small river. It was a time of day when only the most desperate and daring of man-eaters would be likely to show itself.

Pausing for a moment to wipe the sweat from his brow,

Bisnu glanced up at the hillside, and his eye caught sight of a rock on the brown of the hill which seemed unfamiliar to him. Just as he was about to look elsewhere, the round rock began to grow and then alter its shape, and Bisnu watching in fascination was at last able to make out the head and forequarters of the panther. It looked enormous from the angle at which he saw it, and for a moment he thought it was a tiger. But Bisnu knew instinctively that it was the man-eater.

Slowly, the wary beast pulled itself to its feet and began to walk round the side of the great rock. For a second it disappeared and Bisnu wondered if it had gone away. Then it reappeared and the boy was all excitement again. Very slowly and silently the panther walked across the face of the rock until it was in direct line with the corner of the field where Puja was working.

With a thrill of horror Bisnu realized that the panther was stalking his sister. He shook himself free from the spell which had woven itself round him and shouting hoarsely ran forward.

'Run, Puja, run!' he called. 'It's on the hill above you!'

Puja turned to see what Bisnu was shouting about. She saw him gesticulate to the hill behind her, looked up just in time to see the panther crouching for his spring.

With great presence of mind, she leapt down the banking of the field and tumbled into an irrigation ditch.

The springing panther missed its prey, lost its foothold on the slippery shale banking and somersaulted into the ditch a few feet away from Puja. Before the animal could recover from its surprise, Bisnu was dashing down the slope, swinging his axe and shouting, '*Maro, maro!* (Kill, kill!)

Two men came running across the field. They, too, were armed with axes. Together with Bisnu they made a half-circle around the snarling animal, which turned at bay and plunged at them in order to get away. Puja wriggled along the ditch on her stomach. The men aimed their axes at the panther's head, and Bisnu had the satisfaction of getting in a well-aimed blow between the eyes. The animal then charged straight at one of the men, knocked him over and tried to get at his throat. Just then Sanjay's father arrived with his long spear. He plunged the end of the spear into the panther's neck.

The panther left its victim and ran into the bushes, dragging the spear through the grass and leaving a trail of blood on the ground. The men followed cautiously—all except the man who had been wounded and who lay on the ground, while Puja and the other womenfolk rushed up to help him.

The panther had made for the bed of the stream and Bisnu, Sanjay's father and their companion were able to follow it quite easily. The water was red where the panther had crossed the stream, and the rocks were stained with blood. After they had gone downstream for about a furlong, they found the panther lying still on its side at the edge of the water. It was mortally wounded, but it continued to wave its tail like an angry cat. Then, even the tail lay still.

'It is dead,' said Bisnu. 'It will not trouble us again in this body.'

'Let us be certain,' said Sanjay's father, and he bent down and pulled the panther's tail.

There was no response.

'It is dead,' said Kalam Singh. 'No panther would suffer such an insult were it alive!'

They cut down a long piece of thick bamboo and tied the panther to it by its feet. Then, with their enemy hanging upside down from the bamboo pole, they started back for the village.

'There will be a feast at my house tonight,' said Kalam

Singh. 'Everyone in the village must come. And tomorrow we will visit all the villages in the valley and show them the dead panther, so that they may move about again without fear.'

'We can sell the skin in Kemptee,' said their companion. 'It will fetch a good price.'

'But the claws we will give to Bisnu,' said Kalam Singh, putting his arm around the boy's shoulders. 'He has done a man's work today. He deserves the claws.'

A panther's or tiger's claws are considered to be lucky charms.

'I will take only three claws,' said Bisnu. 'One each for my mother and sister, and one for myself. You may give the others to Sanjay and Chittru and the smaller children.'

As the sun set, a big fire was lit in the middle of the village of Manjari and the people gathered round it, singing and laughing. Kalam Singh killed his fattest goat and there was meat for everyone.

## IX

Bisnu was on his way home. He had just handed in his first paper, arithmetic, which he had found quite easy. Tomorrow it would be algebra, and when he got home he would have to practice square roots and cube roots and fractional coefficients.

Mr Nautiyal and the entire class had been happy that he had been able to sit for the exams. He was also a hero to them for his part in killing the panther. The story had spread through the villages with the rapidity of a forest fire, a fire which was now raging in Kemptee town.

When he walked past the hospital, he was whistling cheerfully. Dr Taylor waved to him from the verandah steps.

'How is Sanjay now?' she asked.

'He is well,' said Bisnu.

'And your mother and sister?'

'They are well,' said Bisnu.

'Are you going to get yourself a new dog?'

'I am thinking about it,' said Bisnu. 'At present I have a baby goat—I am teaching it to swim!'

He started down the path to the valley. Dark clouds had gathered and there was a rumble of thunder. A storm was imminent.

'Wait for me!' shouted Sarru, running down the path behind Bisnu, his milk pails clanging against each other. He fell into step beside Bisnu.

'Well, I hope we don't have any more man-eaters for some time,' he said. 'I've lost a lot of money by not being able to take milk up to Kemptee.'

'We should be safe as long as a shikari doesn't wound another panther. There was an old bullet wound in the man-eater's thigh. That's why it couldn't hunt in the forest. The deer were too fast for it.'

'Is there a new postman yet?'

'He starts tomorrow. A cousin of Mela Ram's.'

When they reached the parting of their ways it had begun to rain a little.

'I must hurry,' said Sarru. 'It's going to get heavier any minute.' 'I feel like getting wet,' said Bisnu. 'This time it's the monsoon, I'm sure.'

Bisnu entered the forest on his own, and at the same time the rain came down in heavy opaque sheets. The trees shook in the wind, the langoors chattered with excitement.

It was still pouring when Bisnu emerged from the forest, drenched to the skin. But the rain stopped suddenly, just as the village of Manjari came in view. The sun appeared through a rift in the clouds. The leaves and the grass gave out a sweet, fresh smell.

Bisnu could see his mother and sister in the field transplanting the rice seedlings. The menfolk were driving the yoked oxen through the thin mud of the fields, while the children hung on to the oxen's tails, standing on the plain wooden harrows and with weird cries and shouts sending the animals almost at a gallop along the narrow terraces.

Bisnu felt the urge to be with them, working in the fields. He ran clown the path, his feet falling softly on the wet earth. Puja saw him coming and waved to him. She met him at the edge of the field.

'How did you find your paper today?' she asked.

'Oh, it was easy.' Bisnu slipped his hand into hers and together they walked across the field. Puja felt something smooth and hard against her fingers, and before she could see what Bisnu was doing, he had slipped a pair of bangles over her wrist.

'I remembered,' he said, with a sense of achievement. Puja looked at the bangles and burst out: 'But they are blue, Bhai, and I wanted red and gold bangles!' And then, when she saw him looking crestfallen, she hurried on: 'But they are very pretty, and you did remember... Actually, they're just as nice as red and gold bangles! Come into the house when you are ready. I have made something special for you.'

'I am coming,' said Bisnu, turning towards the house. 'You don't know how hungry a man gets, walking five miles to reach home!'